My first book is for Geoff.
His hat is awesome.

E. L.

First published in the UK in 2017 by Nosy Crow Ltd
The Crow's Nest, 14 Baden Place, Crosby Row
London, SE1 1YW, UK

Nosy Crow and associated logos are trademarks and/or registered
trademarks of Nosy Crow Ltd

Printed and bound in the UK by Clays Ltd, St. Ives Plc

Papers used by Nosy Crow are made from wood grown in
sustainable forests.

ISBN: 978 1 7880 0013 0

www.nosycrow.com

# You Can't Make Me Go To Witch School!

# EM LYNAS

illustrated by JAMIE LITTLER

nosy crow

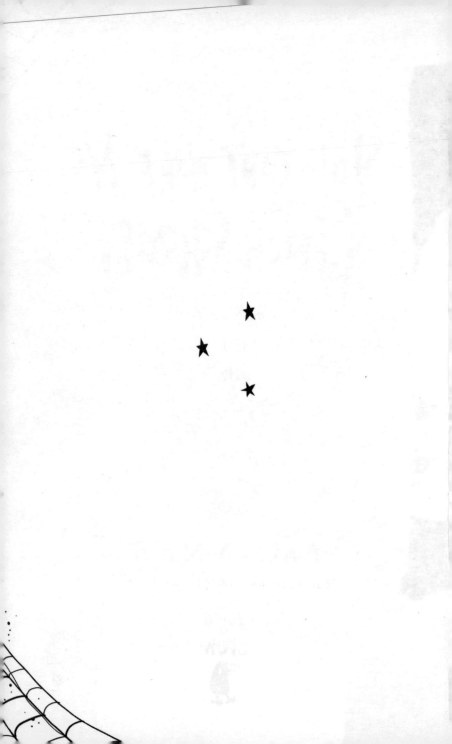

**DAISY WART** is a Shakespearean actress, not a witch, and must escape from Toadspit Towers, School for Witches, in order to perform her Bottom.

*My name is Daisy Wart and I am currently living in the land of SERIOUSLY ANNOYED! I am being DUMPED at Toadspit Towers, School for Witches, by my granny even though I am definitely, positively, absolutely not a WITCH. I am an ACTRESS!*

★

Granny Wart pushes me towards the school steps with her broomstick. She's a traditional witch: black cloak, black hat, and red in the face if she doesn't get her own way. But she's cuddly too. Like a pile of cushions in a dress.

I'm neither cuddly nor skinny. I'm in between. Granny says my face is the sort of face that people smile at. In a good way. That my green eyes remind her of her favourite nettle tea, but my hair is annoying,

like conker-brown brambles. Normally.

I'm currently hiding my hair from the world under my new woolly birthday hat that is green and yellow and stripy. There are earflaps and pompoms. It's my favourite hat ever and I will probably never ever take it off even though it does not match my birthday dress, which is blue with daisies, or my green boots, which match my eyes. My socks are purple.

"Go on then," she says. "Get in there. It's your birthday treat. Happy eleventh."

Birthday treat? I disagree. We're standing in front of a derelict building. The sun is going down and the shadows are growing but I can still see the place is crumbly. Weeds are growing out of cracks. Old roots are pushing up through the grass, climbing up the brickwork and surrounding the door frame.

"Granny." I say it with firmness. This is definitely a hands-on-hips moment, so I put them there. "Chocolate, currently in my backpack, is a birthday treat. *The Complete Works of William Shakespeare* with pictures, also currently in my backpack, is a

3

birthday treat. Money, in the backpack, is a birthday treat. Dumping me at witch school is NOT a birthday treat. I absolutely refuse to enter a dilapidated building named Toadspit Towers because I am NOT a witch!"

This is now a moment of determination, a folding-of-the-arms moment, so I do fold them. I add in a glare. I'm rather good at glares.

Granny tuts and jabs me again. "For goodness' sake, child. Stop your play-acting. You is a witch cos I knows you is a witch. I sees your hat. Tis proof. Now, knock on that door knocker before I poke your bottom one more time!"

She shakes her broomstick at me but I don't step forward because I am thinking there is NO WAY that I am touching *that* knocker on that door. *That* knocker is a gargoyle's head and it just scowled at me. It has teeth. It's gnashing them. Fingers and thumbs could be lost and I like my fingers and thumbs. They're useful.

We both jump when the gargoyle knocker says, in

a voice of doom, "Be you witches?"

"Aye," says Granny. She drags me up the steps. She is surprisingly strong for a granny. "We be two witches."

"One," says I, loudly.

"Two," says Granny, even louder.

"Prove it," says the knocker.

Granny nips the gargoyle's lips shut and bangs his chin on the wood. Three loud knocks echo in the building. She lets go and his mouth springs open.

"Proof enough?" says Granny.

The gargoyle nods crossly and stretches his lips back into shape as the knocks continue to echo through the school. The sounds die away to silence.

"See. There's no one here," I say. I take a step back and inspect the building. A line of bats escape into the autumn twilight through a broken window, high up in the tower on the right. "Look, even the bats are leaving. They've probably closed the school because all the witches have died and gone to witchy heaven." I put my arm round her shoulders. "I'll do you a deal. Let's go home and I'll make you a nice cup of your very own Calming Nettle Tea, in bed, every morning for a month, and you can forget all about Toadspit Towers."

I think she's giving in but then, to my ginormous disappointment and her ginormous joy, the door creaks open slowly like in a scary monster movie.

*Creak, creak, creak.*

I'm thinking Dracula, Frankenstein's monster, werewolf...

It isn't.

In the gloomy doorway there's a woman with a wooden leg. The left one. It's pale, like pine, with a golden grain running through. I'm guessing she's a witch but she doesn't look anything like Granny. She's dressed in a smart, short red dress. Blood red. There's a thick black belt nipping in her waist and a red witchy hat perched precisely on top of her short black hair. The hat is smooth and silky, not like Granny's; hers is rough like hessian and a bit bent at the top.

A silver charm bracelet slides down the woman's wrist as she taps her pointy crimson fingernails on the door. The gargoyle shudders. I think her wooden knee is looking at me. There's a knot on each side;

they look like eyes. One winks. Or maybe it just twitches.

The woman gives us a look. Not a look from the book called *If Looks Could Kill*. This is a look from the book called *If Looks Could Shrivel*. Luckily, she's focusing on Granny Wart. Not me. Not yet.

"Is you the headmistress?" asks Granny. "Is you Ms Toadspit?"

"I am not," says the woman. "I am Ms Constance Thorn. Senior Teacher of Toadspit Towers. You may speak."

Granny pulls me up the last step. "I has a witch for you. She's special. Extra special. I feels it in me bones and me bones are never wrong, especially me elbows. Tis her destiny to be—"

Ms Thorn interrupts in a bored voice. "Ah, yes. Destiny." She switches her look to me and inspects me from toe to top. She narrows her eyes when she gets to my hat. I don't think she likes it. Her charm bracelet jingles, even though she isn't moving her hand. It jingles again and, without taking her eyes off

me, she unhooks a charm with her other hand. It's a tiny silver bat then, suddenly, it's a real bat. It hangs off her ear as if it's whispering something.

I can't tell what the witchy teacher's thinking because her face is blank of emotional information. Like a statue. The bat drops down to her shoulder and she says, "You may enter the hallowed halls of education. Where we nurture the minds and *mumble* the bodies."

The mumble sounds like "torture" but that can't be right. I back away. Granny pushes me and I am propelled reluctantly through the door into a musty, dusty entrance hall.

"Don't mind if I do enter in," says Granny, following. "Let's have a nice cuppa tea an' a shortbread biscuit while we has a chat about the girl's future."

"Actually," says Ms Thorn, before Granny's foot gets over the threshold. She says it slowly, ac-chew-ally. I memorise the way she says it, which is what actresses do. "I was not inviting you in. Just the girl."

The door slams in Granny's face before Granny can say *BUT*!

"Let me in," shouts Granny, banging on the outside of the door.

"Let me out," shouts me, banging on the inside.

I hear a *squeal*, a *squeak*, and an *eek* from Granny then her footsteps crunch rapidly down the driveway. "Get away from me," she's screaming. "Get away from me. You can't eat me, you monsters! I'm a witch!"

Great piles of dungpats! Granny's ac-chew-ally

running away and LEAVING ME HERE. Which I just CANNOT BELIEVE.

"Thou has just made a BIG mistake," I say to Ms Thorn, doing my best Shakespearean acting. I fold my arms to confirm this. "A very, very, BIG mistake."

"I never make mistakes," she answers. She taps her leg with her cane. "Terrible things happen if one makes mistakes. You will follow me."

Then, just when I'm all fired up for an argument and raring to say there is no way I am going to follow her, she turns away and walks off, taking the light with her. It shines down from the brim of her hat. She looks like a walking lamp stand.

I am left all alone in the darkness of the big, scary, draughty entrance hall. I do not move. I shall not move until they let me out.

The door snarls.

3

I give in. I run after Ms Thorn but after a few steps something tugs me back by my ear. I yelp and spin round but there's nothing there, just dark shadows. Spooky shadows with a tinge of green. Then there's a draught and a ghostly whisper.

It says, "My rules, school rules, never, ever break rules. No running."

My ear is released. I hold my breath and walk. That quick sort of a walk that isn't running. Ms Thorn looks back. She stops and shines her light on me as a tornado of green mist whooshes past me. It spins on to her outstretched palm. The mist takes shape. It changes into a wooden doll wearing an emerald dress and a matching hat. Her shiny black hair is pulled back into a bun and there's a tiny charm bracelet dangling around her neck. There's only one charm, a tarnished silver tree.

The doll raises one arm and points at me. "New girl, new girl, who are you? Say your name and tell me true." I hear it even though its mouth doesn't move.

I stammer out my name. "D-d-daisy Wart."

The doll changes back to mist and spins off down the corridor sighing, "Alas, just a Wart, a Toadspit Wart…" Her voice disappears along with the mist.

"What was that?" I ask Ms Thorn. My voice has gone all squeaky.

"That was Ms Toadspit," says Ms Thorn. "Our esteemed headmistress. Despite her death." She points to a dusty portrait on the wall. The witch has a vague resemblance to the doll but looks much younger. Her hair is loose and she's smiling. The title under the picture is *Ms Ursula Toadspit, Headmistress and Founder of Toadspit Towers. 1642–1728–now.*

I gulp. "The headmistress is a ghost?"

Ms Thorn walks on, taking the light. "She is.

Conform and comply with Ms Toadspit's rules and all will be well," she says over her shoulder.

No it won't! I don't want to comply. I want to go home. Unfortunately, I have no option but to follow the teacher and her witchy light.

There are more dusty pictures all along the corridors. Old witches in old clothes. I watch them carefully as I go past. I think they're watching me. Ms Thorn's cane *tap, tap, taps* on the flagstones and her wooden leg goes *thunk, thunk, thunk* in between. The bat is riding on her shoulder, watching me. I name it Fangus.

We stop at a yellow door. The shiny brass plaque says *Ms Sage, Deputy Headmistress*. There's a tree root growing up between the flagstones on either side, the same colour as Ms Thorn's leg, pale with golden streaks. Each root is twisted into intricate knots and Celtic patterns.

I touch one. "Ouch!" Ms Thorn looks down. I show her my bleeding thumb. "It pricked me!"

She is not sympathetic. "You have been tested by

the witchwood," she says as she knocks the door's gargoyle knocker and goes in without waiting. I follow, sucking my thumb to stop the bleeding. If I don't explain to someone in power that I MUST LEAVE IMMEDIATELY I may just burst.

We enter a library. Books are stuffed on the shelves and stacked in wobbly piles on the floor. I guess we're in a Toadspit tower because the walls are curved. The wall on the right is covered in mirrors. Big, small and in between with silver, gold and wooden frames. There's a wooden spiral staircase on the left and a really low desk and a comfy chair with purple cushions in the middle.

At first I think the room is empty but then there's a metallic clunk that makes me jump and I see a very short witch standing on tiptoes at a contraption of brass and glass tubes. There's a plaque at the top with the words *The Communicator* engraved.

Ms Thorn says, "Excuse the interruption, Ms Sage. We have a new pupil."

The witch turns to look at us. She's about my

height but chubbier. Her dress is orange with stars and moons embroidered in blue. It stops above her ankles, revealing pink bunny slippers. Her hat is yellow, like warm, old gold. It's covered in swirls of velvet and lace, twisted, plaited and knotted.

Ms Thorn puts a hand on my shoulder. "Daisy Wart. Delivered into our care by her granny who insists she is 'special', but don't they all?"

This is my opportunity. I load my voice with politeness and firmness and prepare to ad lib a *Let Me Out of Here* speech.

"Good evening, Ms Sage. My granny has made an enormous mistake. This is a school for witches and I am NOT a witch. I am an ACTRESS. A Shakespearian actress. I have an extremely important performance in exactly two sleeps and I must be allowed to leave immediately."

I am ac-chew-ally playing the part of Bottom in *A Midsummer Night's Dream*, even though Bottom is a man with a donkey's head and I, of course, am a girl not a man and do not have a donkey's head. But she

doesn't need to know any of that. I continue.

"Kindly show me back to the front door." I pause and say, "And open it." Then, just to be absolutely clear, I add, "And let me out."

This is definitely another hands-on-hips moment so I put them there to emphasise my previously mentioned firmness and determination.

The ears on Ms Sage's bunny slippers flip and flap as she walks to her desk. A big black book floats out of a bookcase and lands in front of her. It opens. A pen dips into the inkwell and hovers over the book. Ms Sage leans forward with her hands palm down on the desk. She knocks the inkpot with her elbow, making it spin as she peers at me over the top of her glasses. She looks slightly puzzled, as if she's scanned me and hasn't quite got all the information she needs.

Fangus squeaks and Ms Thorn says, "Felix feels her power."

Hm, Fangus is a Felix. I prefer my name for him. It's more descriptive.

"How marvellous," says Ms Sage. She flicks her sleeve back and reveals a silver charm bracelet like Ms Thorn's, only this one is packed tight with charms. "I shall ask Horatio to confirm." She unhooks a charm and an owl appears on her shoulder. It's a tiny owl with fluffed-up brown feathers. It stares at me with its big wise-owl eyes.

It stares. I stare. It stares. I stare. It stares. I stare. I

can play this game forever. My record with Granny is one hour, twenty-seven minutes, thirteen seconds and a nanosecond. The nano is important because that's when you win.

The owl looks away. He hoots at Ms Sage. She nods. Now she's smiling at me as if I'm a box of chocolates. "Horatio feels her witch power too and yet …" she peers at my head again, "… I see no hat."

She must be blind, I think. You can't *not* see my hat. It's on my head. I'm just about to demand a phone call when she stares at me again and goes cross-eyed.

She whispers something under her breath and her eyes uncross. She's clapping her hands like a sea lion. "There it is! Every witch has a witch's hat and yours is sitting on top of your head but it is rather indistinct. A ghost of a hat. A fog of a hat. Nevertheless, it is definitely a hat."

She's obviously confused. "This is not a witchy hat," I say, pulling the pompoms down. "This is a woolly hat knitted by my granny, who *she*," I point at Ms Thorn, "would not let through the door."

Ms Sage looks at me kindly. "Not *that* hat, dear. Your witch's hat. It is revealed on your eleventh birthday. Your hat is you. You are your hat. You just can't see it yet." She squints at me again with her cross-eyed eyes. Her eyebrows squeeze together above her nose. "But what colour, Horatio? Is it green for a seventh child? Or orange for a seventh child of a seventh child? Or purple for a seventh of a seventh of a seventh?" She squints even more. The owl goes cross-eyed too. "Yellow, red, blue … it's hard to tell. There's constant movement. Constant change. As if it hasn't quite decided what it wants to be."

Horatio hoots again. Ms Sage's eyes focus and her face lights up.

"Oh, well done, Horatio!" she says, then she smiles at me. "Horatio has found your real name from your deepest memories. You are…" She listens to the owl.

"Winkle … Crinkle … Tinkle…"

21

"Twinkle! Your name is Twinkle," she declares. "But Twinkle who?"

Horatio shrugs his feathers as if he doesn't know. Ms Sage doesn't seem to mind. "Ah, well, I'm sure we'll find out eventually. Now, my dear, you just need to say your name three times – Twinkle, Twinkle, Twinkle – and your hat will be revealed to you and everyone else." She waits.

I will not! That's a ridiculous name. "You are mistaken, Ms Sage," I say. "My name is not that name. My name is Daisy Wart." I'd much rather be a Daisy than a Twinkle. "I absolutely do not possess a witchy hat because I am not a witch. This is a case of mistaken identity. Please could you call me a taxi? I need to go home at once."

"Oh, I can't possibly do that, dear," she says sweetly. "Your granny gave you into our care. We are now responsible for you."

The pen hovering over the big black book dips into the inkwell again and makes a scratchy noise as it writes something halfway down the page. There's a big grin on Ms Sage's face, as if she's won a prize and that prize is me.

"There we are, my dear. It's official. Your name is in the ledger. Toadspit Towers is the oldest witch school in the world and it is now your home until you graduate at eighteen. We're so pleased you came to us."

I am SPEECHLESS with shock! I'm beyond acting calm or firm or grown up, and I splutter, "But I'm not a witch! I'm an actress! This is kidnapping!"

"Oh, how dramatic," says Ms Sage. "How perfectly entertaining." A clock chimes from somewhere in the bookcases.

"Eight o'clock," says Ms Thorn.

"So late," says Ms Sage to me. "I have much to do

and you must be tired."

"I am not," I say firmly.

She smiles at me. It's an odd smile. Her head tilts to the side. Her eyebrows lift a little and her grey eyes sparkle. "You really *must* be tired, Twinkle. Going to bed is *definitely* the *sensible* thing to do." Her smile is a smile of certainty. As if she doesn't expect me to refuse her sensible suggestion.

I wasn't tired but now, all of a sudden, I am. I imagine a cosy bed with a fluffy duvet and pillows. Ms Sage is right. I will *definitely* feel better after a good night's sleep.

"This way," says Ms Thorn. I follow her through dark corridor after dark corridor. I'm sleepy and gloomy and yawning. I'm suffering from gloomitus and the only cure is escape. But not now. I yawn some more.

We turn rights and lefts and lefts and rights and I have no idea where I am. I need a map. I yawn again. I can't stop. We climb a set of narrow stairs and go along a dark and dismal corridor. We pass

dusty doors and dodge dangly cobwebs. We climb again. We turn a corner. It's a bit cleaner. Not much. There are brass cat knockers on the doors. Ms Thorn stops. I almost bump into her.

"Your dormitory," she says. "You are now a Junior Witch, year one, dormitory four."

The door creaks open. I am shocked out of my sleepiness mid-yawn. I don't see a Victorian dormitory with rows of beds and chamber pots, which would fit in so well with the rest of the crumbly building.

Oh, no.

I see giant cauldrons. Seven cauldrons hanging from the ceiling by metal chains. Seven sinks on the left and three high arched windows at the back. The cauldron at the front has a big yellow rosette hanging from its chain. It says B&B in the centre. Does that mean bed and breakfast? Are these cauldrons ac-chew-ally beds?

Ms Thorn taps a cauldron and a rope ladder unrolls from the top. "This is yours," she says.

"You have to be kidding me!" I say. The tired feeling has completely gone. I am wide awake and my determination to leave has returned. "I refuse to sleep in a cauldron. I am a normal person and I always sleep in a normal bed. In my own home!"

"Home is where the heart is," says Ms Thorn. She

touches my chest with a red pointy fingernail. "And your heart is here. Sleep in the cauldron. Sleep on the floor. It is your choice. Comply and conform and all will be well."

She leaves me in the dark. Again. I push at the door but it's locked and the handle won't budge. I slump to the floorboards; they're really hard on my bottom. Moonlight shines through the window and my eyes slowly adjust. There's a cat sitting next to the door. It's smooth and pale, like the witchwood. I think it's waiting to be let out. Me too.

I am starring in a tragedy of tragickness! My life is a dung heap of smelliness and I'm stuck right in the middle of it until I think of a way out. Everything is as bad as it can be. It can't possibly get any worse.

Suddenly there's a light in the darkness and someone says, "Good evening."

The light's coming from the cauldron with the B&B rosette on. There's a girl's head poking out. A slightly smaller version of Ms Thorn's smooth and silky red hat is perched on top of her tight, black curly hair, which is cut short. Her face is long and thin.

"I am Dominique Laffitte," says the girl without smiling. "You are new."

*Well, that's stating the obvious*, I think. So I say nothing. Dominique doesn't seem to need me to say anything anyway because she keeps talking as she climbs out of the cauldron. She's wearing pyjamas covered in cats.

"Ms Thorn has appointed I dormitory monitor for I am the Best and Brightest Witch." She points at the rosette on her cauldron as proof. "I have knowledge of everything in this school. If there is anything you want to know then ask I. And if there is anything you should know then I shall tell you. And if there is anything you do wrong, I shall tell you that too. You are lucky to be sharing the dormitory of the youngest Best and Brightest Witch in the history of Toadspit Towers. Ms Thorn says that I will be the Best and Brightest every year until I leave because there is no one better than I in the whole school. I am the seventh girl child of a seventh girl child of a…"

*Blah, blah, blah.* I act interested because she might know the way out. "How many was that?" I ask politely, when I realise she's stopped talking.

"Five generations." She says it very proudly. "You can see that from my hat. It is red. There are only ten girls in this school with a red hat."

"How marvellous for you," I say. I act sincere.

She knocks on the two cauldrons behind hers. *Thunk. Thunk.* A head appears on the left then another on the right. It reminds me of one of those games, where you whack the gopher on the head with a foam mallet.

"This is Arwen." Dominique points to the girl with long, wavy auburn hair. Her hat is red too, but not the same red as Dominique's. It's darker, duller. "You must introduce yourself to the new girl, Arwen."

Arwen flicks her hair over her shoulder and looks down on me. Her freckly nose is a bit podgy, like a strawberry. "I am Arwen of Aberystwyth," she says. "My mother is Alis of Aberystwyth. My grandmother is Ariana of Aberdovey. My great-grandmother was Angharad, the Old Mother of Aberdare." She says this as if I would have heard of them. Like they're some sort of celebrity witch family off the telly. She keeps going. I stop listening until Dominique points to the other girl.

"This is Shalini Chandra," she says. Shalini is petite and neat with big brown eyes and a long black ponytail. "She is just a seventh girl child, as you can see from her green hat," says Dominique. "She is quite new too. She arrived one month and two weeks ago."

Shalini's hat is different shades of green, like Granny's nettles in the sunshine. The brim flops down, hiding one eye. Her charm bracelet slides up her wrist as she wiggles her fingers in a wave of hello and I realise that all the girls have one.

They both climb down and join Dominique. She leans over me. "And now you," she says. She's squinting at my head. "Who are you? What is your history? Where is your hat?"

Hm. *Who am I?* Suddenly Daisy Wart doesn't sound interesting enough and I am certainly not going to say the name that Ms Sage named me, which is the world's most ridiculous name and will never leave my lips. As I'm in a tragedy, I pick the most tragic Shakespearean name I can think of.

"Ophelia," I say in a voice full of sadness. "My name is Ophelia, I am a Shakespearean actress from Stratford upon Avon." That's not true, the bit about Stratford. "I'm not a witch. I have been kidnapped." That's true.

"Ophelia," says Dominique, ignoring the fact I've been kidnapped. She stretches out the name like this, Oooooofeeeeelia, and I wish I'd chosen Desdemona instead. But she would have probably said Desdemooooooona so maybe something ordinary like Juliet would have done. But no, she could have said Joooooliet. Are no names safe from this girl! But what's in a name, I remind myself. For I shall be gone anon, as Master Shakespeare would say. I don't need to make friends. I just need to get out. I act my best smile for them all.

"Yes. Ophelia. Upon my honour, I am not a witch and if someone could just show me the way out then I shall leave immediately. I have a very important performance to get ready for."

"You cannot possibly leave," says Dominique. It's like an order. "Not at night."

I HATE it when people use the CANNOT word.

"Why not?" I say. I act not cross.

Arwen leans forward and says in an *I shall scare you with stories of scary stuff* voice, "Because of the Toadspit Terrors."

"Yes," says Shalini. Her voice is high and squeaky. "The big beasties stalk the corridors at night. If you listen really carefully you can hear them scuttling past at the dead of darkness." Shalini looks nervously at the door. "Sometimes the scuttling stops," she says. "*Just outside the door!*"

"They have great big claws," says Arwen, with her scary voice. "And great big jaws and great big gruesome goggly eyes. They gobble up normals."

"But not witches," says Shalini quickly.

They have to be making this up! Don't they? I groan and hug my knees to my chest.

"I can't believe this is happening. Granny dumped

me here because she thinks I'm a witch. Now Ms Sage thinks I'm a witch. And Ms Thorn. But I'm not. I'm really not. I don't feel at all witchy. And everything here is so dark and cobwebby and scary with ghostly headmistresses and Terrible Terrors and now I have to sleep in a cauldron, which will be cold and hard and horrible, and it's ac-chew-ally my birthday."

My voice catches on the word birthday and I think I'm about to burst into tears in front of these girls who I don't know at all.

"Oh, poor you," says Shalini, patting me on the shoulder.

"You are ignorant," says Dominique, which, frankly, is so RUDE that I stop feeling sorry for myself and feel cross instead. She keeps talking. "Cauldrons are far better than beds. You may see mine. To see the cauldron of the Best and Brightest Witch of the Year will give you something to remember when you are back with the normals. A memory of all that could have been if you actually had been a witch such as

I."

I have no idea how she keeps her hat on her head, it is so big. The head, not the hat.

They all climb into Dominique's cauldron leaving me on the hard floor. I decide to follow but it's not easy climbing up a rope ladder. I'm an actress, not an athlete. I reach the top and peep in.

"WOW!"

Granny HAS to make me a cauldron bed.

6

"Wow," I repeat to myself. Inside the cauldron is HUGE.

Golden light is shining from the padded walls and the girls are glowing with it. They're sitting on a thick duvet and comfy cushions, covered in jazzy African prints of orange and blue. Dominique looks very pleased at my reaction. She almost smiles as she explains.

"The witches of Toadspit Towers use spare space. They channel the witchwood to control all the spare space between the atoms and move it to where they want it. Only the best witches are able to do this on a grand scale. Our whole school was built by witches using spare space. This will be difficult for a normal to understand."

Of course I understand. I'm not stupid. I feel the cauldron stretch a bit as I climb down the ladder. The walls are covered in awards, certificates and rosettes. Best witch at this, best witch at that, best witch at everything in witchland.

I like awards. I have a space on my dressing table ready for my first Oscar. I've made one out of play dough to keep the spot.

"We shall have cake," says Dominique. "We shall show Ophelia how good witches share." She presses a patch on the wall and it opens. There's a huge chocolate cake inside a cubbyhole, plus three flowery china plates and a knife.

"I do not have plates for all," she says. "Someone will have no cake. Shalini, it will be you. You will be a kind witch and give up your cake for Ophelia."

I suddenly realise what B&B really stands for. Biggest and Bossiest.

Shalini smiles at me and says, "Oh yes. That's fine. It's Ophelia's birthday, after all. I don't mind. Really I don't."

But she does. Who wouldn't?

"We could share the plate," I say.

"No," says Dominique. "She will drop crumbs."

"She always drops crumbs," says Arwen.

They are not being fair. I remember the birthday treat in my backpack. "Aha!" I say. "I have chocolate. You can have that instead, Shalini." I hand it over. "Chocolate has no crumbs."

Shalini looks to Dominique as if she's asking for permission. I push it into her hand. "Eat it later if you don't want it now," I say. She puts it in her pocket.

Dominique cuts the thinnest slice of cake possible and hands it to me. Honestly, if I could hold it up to the light I would see through it. I suddenly wish I'd kept some of the chocolate for me. Arwen tucks her hair behind her ears and takes her piece. It's a little bit thicker than mine. Dominique cuts a big slice for herself.

"So," says Arwen, taking a tiny bite. "Why does your granny think you're a witch?"

Dominique tuts at her. "Arwen, a better question would be – if Ophelia is not a witch then why did Ms Sage allow Ophelia to stay at Toadspit Towers? Or, where is Ophelia from? Or, who does Ophelia think she is?" She takes a big bite of cake. Everyone waits for me to respond.

Aha! An audience! All the world's a stage, even in a cauldron.

"Well. I don't really know where I'm from. But

Granny used to tell me this story of how she found me." I put on a scary witchy voice, like the witches in *Macbeth*, who are all hubbly and bubbly and toily and troubly. I bend over a bit, old-lady-like, and tell the tale exactly as Granny tells it. I have an excellent memory. I'm an actress.

"Once upon a dark and dismal night of rain and thunder and heavy skies an old woman was a-walking by a hedgerow. She had a hankering for an eye-of-newt and toe-of-toad omelette for supper and was a-searching the dank and rank ditches and puddles of the Fen Ley when all of a sudden she heard a baby's cry.

"'Lawks a mercy!' said the old woman. 'Be that a baby? But what be a baby doing outside on a night of drenching rain and thunder?' She poked about with her broomstick and cleared away the grass and cow parsley. 'By my broom!' cried the witch. 'Tis a baby! A baby in a basket. Why, tis the prettiest baby girl I ever did see.'"

I change the last bit. Granny always says "the

ugliest baby girl ever, with her face all screwed up and red from crying".

"'Has anyone lost a baby?' called the old woman into the blackest darkness, but her words were carried away by the wind and no one answered. So the old woman picked up the basket, baby and all, and took the child home to raise as her own. They lived happily ever after in a cottage in the woods and no one ever knew that the child was not her very own grandchild."

Shalini looks ready to cry so I must have told it well.

"Granny's quite famous," I say. "She makes Nervous Nelly's Nettle Therapies. For anxiety. It's sold in all the best alternative medicine shops." This is true. I sing the jingle. "When your knees are a-knocking and your belly is a-jelly, you can cure the nervy fretting with a sip of Nervous Nelly."

I don't think they've heard it before.

I try, "Don't bother with psychology, just sip a Calming Cuppa Tea." They haven't heard that before either. I give up. "I go to St Bluebottle's. I'm in year six and I have to get out of here as soon as possible because I have to perform my—"

"Quiet," says Dominique. Which, again, is so rude.

The cauldron swings, as if someone or something is climbing the ladder. Dominique clucks her tongue in annoyance like this: *tsk*.

A girl appears. She has a round face and a big smile. Her hair is bobbed, with a fringe. It's as brown and shiny as the icing on the chocolate cake. Her hat is green like Shalini's but it's splattered with every shade of green imaginable, as if she's thrown paint at it. It's rough and smooth and dented in places. There's a lopsided lacy bow on the front and a fluffy feather trailing behind.

"What's happen— Hey, a new girl," she says, spotting me. Her eyes light up at the sight of the cake. "Ooh, cake. My mam can't bake cakes. They go flat in the middle and come out like biscuits. But that's OK because I like biscuits. And pie."

Dominique ignores her and puts the spare cake away in the cubbyhole as Arwen says, "This is Ophelia, Jessica. She's just arrived. This is Jessica Moss," she says to me.

"You can call me Jess," says the girl. "It's quicker."

And that's it. No one tells me how many witchy ancestors Jessica Moss has. Or where she's from. Or anything. I briefly wonder what Jess has done to annoy Miss Besty Witch but then decide it's not my business. I'm leaving tomorrow.

Shalini cranes her neck back. "Ophelia isn't a witch, Jessica, she's a Shakespearean actress. It's all a big mistake and she won't be stay..." Her voice

trails away as Dominique gives her a look from *The Book of Looks That Mean I Did Not Tell You To Speak.*

Arwen gets to her feet. "We're going to bed. Move, Jessica," she orders.

"Ooooh, the power," says Jess. "I could trap you all in the cauldron like little fishies in a fishbowl." She doesn't though. She grins and disappears, and we climb out. I am secretly pleased to be going to bed. I'm properly tired now and I CANNOT WAIT to get inside my very own cauldron even for one night. I'm thinking fluffy and feathery thoughts. My ladder unfurls and I pause when I reach the top to say a dramatic goodnight but everyone has disappeared except Jess.

"Night, night. Sleep tight. Don't let the bed bugs bite," she says, and climbs into her cauldron.

Bed bugs! There'd better not be bed bugs! I look down into my cauldron and I am suddenly transported into a world of DISAPPOINTMENT!

There's absolutely no sign of downy duvets or

comfy cushions. There's a mattress of extreme thinness and a blanket of shabbiness. I briefly consider sleeping on the floor as a protest but even a mattress of thinness is better than floorboards. I climb in and press all over the iron walls just in case there's a secret compartment stuffed with a comfy duvet and pillows. There isn't.

I pull the blanket over me and use my backpack as a pillow. The walls go dim and dimmer until there is no light and I am alone in the dark again.

As I drift off to sleep, swinging the cauldron like a cradle, I think of escape … and Granny.

### Summary:

*I have been kidnapped by mad witches. I must escape if I am to perform my Bottom and win an Oscar.*

★

I'm woken by something that sounds like a gong. Then I realise I am *in* the gong and someone is banging on the outside of my iron-pot prison with Thor's hammer. Or something just as big and annoying.

*Bong, bong, bong.*

"Stop that!" I yell. The banging stops. I turn on my back and stretch my arms above my head. My arms are wearing cat pyjamas! I throw the blanket off. My entire body is wearing cat pyjamas! Someone has disappeared my clothes and witchified me as I slept.

How dare they! I touch my head. My hair is still hidden under my woolly hat. I check my backpack. Money and book are there too. I consider what to do next. I have thought a lot of thoughts in my sleepy world and I have not ONE but TWO Great Escape Plans.

*Great Escape Plan A: The Find a Map of the School and Secretly Leave Plan is a work in progress.*

*Great Escape Plan B: The Great Stink Bomb Plan. I am the bomb. I shall not wash until they let me go. I shall add to the smell at every opportunity and be out in time to perform.*

A shadow falls over the walls. I look up. It's Jess. "Time for breakfast," she says. "Are you hungry?"

"I'm absolutely starving." I rub my stomach and it gurgles as proof.

"That's a pity," she says, and leaves.

*That's a pity* is not a phrase I like to associate with food. It does not bode well, as Granny would say. If breakfast looks like gruel, I may just faint. Aha! *Great Escape Plan C: The Have Some Sort of Very*

*Small, Tiny, Non-life-threatening Medical Crisis That Would Require an Ambulance Plan.*

Something rustles behind me. A uniform is hanging from a hook that was previously not there. Grey skirt, white shirt, stripy tights and lace-up boots. Plus a black tie printed with white cats. JW1 is embroidered in green on the shirt pocket. I consider staying in the cat pyjamas as an act of defiance. It could be *Great Escape Plan D: Refuse to Get Dressed Until I am Released.*

I'm liking *Great Escape Plan D* a lot until I realise that if I do manage to escape with *Great Escape Plan A, B* or *C* I would be in the outside world in my pyjamas. Which would not be good. So I reluctantly put the uniform on but I don't fasten the top button and I leave the tie loose as an act of defiance. I grab my backpack and climb out.

"This is yours," says Dominique, pointing to the last sink on the left. There's a towel, toothpaste, toothbrush, soap and a hairbrush on the shelf above the sink.

I don't use any of it – washing is not an option – but I do use the toilet that is behind a door marked with the word Toilet. I'm hoping there'll be a window inside, one I can climb out of, but there isn't. When I come out Jess is waving her toothbrush at an impatient Arwen.

"I can't possibly go any faster, Arwen," says Jess. "My mam says I have to brush up and down at least twenty times on each tooth or I could end up a toothless crone before I'm fourteen." She starts brushing again, slowly nodding her head as if she's counting silently. The feather in her hat flicks up and down as she counts.

I'd love to brush my teeth but smelly breath is essential for *Great Escape Plan B.* So I check the rest of the room for escape opportunities.

I dump my backpack on the floor and pull myself up to look out of the window. There's a tangled garden of jungly bushes and plants, redbrick paths and patches of swirly mist. I can hear strange sounds, like spooky, ghostly flutes. I'm hoping this is the

breeze blowing through the branches of the twisted tree in the centre of the garden, and not actual ghosts playing actual flutes. The tree's leaves are dark green and quite dull, even in the sunshine. It needs some of Granny's special compost from the Fen Ley.

There's school on all sides of the garden so if I did climb out I'd have to climb up and over the roof, which is very, very high. I probably won't do that because I AM NOT AN IDIOT. I shall make this *Great Escape Plan Z.*

Dominique is at my side. She's tall enough to see out easily. She just *has* to tell me what she knows. "That is the witchwood tree, planted by Ms Toadspit herself. It is the heart of the Toadspit garden and the the school."

Jess spits into the sink and says, "I heard a rumour that Ms Toadspit trapped the witchwood."

"I say the truth not rumour," says Dominique to me, not Jess. "Legend says, if the tree ever dies, then the school dies too."

"Why is a legend not a rumour?" says Jess. Dominique ignores her.

*Aha! New Great Escape Plan D: Kill the Tree and the School will Die and I will be Free!*

The mist swirls and the tree disappears. The music stops.

"Where's it gone?" I say. Maybe my thought killed it!

"Wherever it wishes," says Dominique. She moves over to the door. "You must line up," she says.

MUST is a word I hate as much as CANNOT but I have to get out of here so I line up behind Shalini, who is behind Arwen, who is behind Dominique. The cat is still waiting to escape. It's ac-chew-ally a wooden cat, not a real cat. It's looking at me. It's twitching its whiskers. I think it's smelling me.

Jess spits into the sink again and lets the water run over her toothbrush. She slowly turns the tap off. She carefully places her toothbrush into an empty glass. She delicately pats her mouth with a towel. Then she lines up behind me but Dominique *tsks* and Arwen says, "You have to go after Shalini, Jess. You always go after Shalini. Ophelia should be last because she's new."

I swap places. I don't care who's first, second or third, or even fourth. I just want to get out of this room and out of this school.

"Turn round," says Dominique. "No looking. No listening."

Everyone turns round except me. I'm now facing Jess, who whispers loudly, "You have to turn around so Dominique can open the door because she is *the Best and Brightest* and the only one with the magical know-how to do it." She nods as if she's very wise. "We could be trapped in here forever if you don't turn round. It's the truth," she says, nodding again. Then she shakes her head as if it isn't.

I act not giggling because Dominique is scowling a look from *The Book of Scowls* and, who knows, I may need her help to get out of here at some point. So I comply.

Dominique opens the door and we all troop out, including the cat. It prowls down the corridor as a green tornado whips towards us from the other direction with a whoosh and a wail. Ms Toadspit whizzes round me.

"Still no hat upon Wart's head? Will it be blue? Or green? Or red?" My top button fastens itself and my tie tightens around my neck. "Proper and prim. Tidy and trim," she says as she strangles me.

I can't breathe. I grab Jess. She grabs me too as Ms Toadspit whirls around her legs. Her socks were round her ankles and now suddenly they're pulled up to her knees. Shalini's hair is dragged out of her ponytail and plaited down her back. Arwen's hat is straightened. Nothing happens to Dominique; she's already perfect. The Toadspit Tornado whizzes off down the corridor, calling back, "So much to do, no time to stop. Get to breakfast, chop, chop, chop!"

I loosen my tie slightly so I can breathe. Dominique shuts the door and suddenly I can't see a thing. If I ever do find an escape map I won't be able to follow it in this much darkness!

"Lights on," says Dominique. The girls' hats light up with different amounts of bright. Dominique's, of course, is the brightest and steadiest. Shalini's is spreading a warm glow over her shoulders, and Jess's hat is bright but it's flickering on and off. Arwen's is the dimmest. It's casting a dull red light over her face, making her look a bit spooky.

"Follow I," says Dominique. "No talking." She

sets off.

I freeze. Dungpats! I've left my backpack by the window. "Dominique," I call after her politely. "Please could you let me back in. I've forgotten my bag."

"You do not need it," she says over her shoulder.

"I do too need it," I shout after her. "I'm going home and I need my book. I need my money. For bus fare!"

She ignores me and goes around a corner. Arwen follows her, pulling Shalini with her. I give in. Hunger forces me to follow them. Jess links arms with me and lights my way with her flickery beam.

"Is it true you're not a witch?" she asks as we go along the corridor.

"Yes," I answer. "I have been kidnapped and must escape."

"How do you know you're not a witch?" she asks as we go down the stairs.

"I feels it in me bones," I answer, thinking of Granny. "Especially me elbows."

"Does Ms Sage know you're not a witch?" she asks as we go along the landing.

"Ms Sage thinks I *am* a witch," I answer. This girl asks a lot of questions! I ask one. Just to interrupt. "Why is the headmistress a ghost?"

"The rumour is, it was a curse," she says dramatically. We go down more stairs. "Ms Toadspit wanted her seventh daughter to take over in 1722 but they had a massive falling-out. The daughter cursed Ms Toadspit to be the headmistress until a different Toadspit took over. But there's never been another Toadspit at Toadspit Towers. So her ghost is stuck in her doll. Why does Ms Sage think you're a witch if you're not?"

We reach the ground floor. Arwen's waiting. She shushes us. "Dominique says you must stop spreading rumours! Everyone knows Ms Toadspit has *chosen* to be the headmistress forever. You are to stop talking or we'll be late."

Jess is about to say something but I interrupt. "It's fine. We'll be quiet." I don't want to answer any more questions anyway.

We walk on in silence. There are witchwood cats stalking every corridor. They're searching for something.

Eventually we reach double doors with the words Dining Hall above them. They're closed. There are roots growing into Celtic knots and patterns around these doors too.

"We are first," says Dominique. She touches the biggest knot in the roots. "I give thanks to the witchwood," she says. The doors open. It's dark in the hall. She turns to me. "Now you. You must respect the witchwood tree through its roots."

I don't want to. Just because she wants me to. And because it pricked me. "I'm not a witch, I'm an actress," I remind her.

"That does not matter," says Dominique. "Even visitors must be polite. Arwen, you will go next."

Arwen steps forward and touches the witchwood. "I give thanks to the witchwood," she says, and steps through the door. The dining hall lights up a little and I hear creaks and groans, as if it's waking up and stretching. Shalini and Jess say their respects and step through. I see more light and hear more creaks. They're all in the dining hall and I'm outside. I need food! I give in.

I touch the witchwood. It's warm. It tingles. It's like dipping my fingers in fizzy lemonade. They're fizzingling. I like it. I say, "I give thanks to the witchwood," and suddenly I feel like doing a happy dance. I feel like singing. I'm grinning. The roots move, the pattern changes, a hand appears. Palm to palm with mine. Like a slow high-five. The fizzingle spreads from my fingers to my head. I feel dizzy.

8

Dominique drags me away. The link is broken and I want to put my hand back.

"Whoa!" says Jess as the witchwood hand disappears into a pattern. "That's never happened before! I think the witchwood likes you."

"It does not," says Dominique, forgetting not to speak to Jess. She moves between me and the door. "The witchwood has no favourites, Jessica." She says it like this: *Jessicarrr*. "It is just being polite to a visitor."

I reluctantly step away from the door of happiness and into the dining hall. It's big and dusty with lots of rickety-looking tables and chairs. One wall is covered floor to ceiling with wooden shelves. There are rows and rows of wooden dolls. There must be thousands. I don't count; that's a guess. It's like a display of dolls through the ages. The words *Witches of Toadspit* are carved into the stonework above, with a tree on either side. The roots make the letters. In an empty space at the top, on the left, there's a big label instead of a doll. It says: Ursula Toadspit.

On the opposite wall there is a small gold board and seven big boards with different-coloured frames. There's a stage at the front and a balcony with windows above. They're thin like the windows in castles, the ones for firing arrows through. So this is not an escape route. I'm not as skinny as an arrow. If I was I'd be dead.

I look behind me. HURRAH AND HUZZAH! There's the escape route! Floor-to-ceiling French doors open to the world! A garden stretching into the distance. A slight breeze is blowing a mix of perfumes into the hall. Honeysuckle, lavender, roses and a lot I don't recognise. I can sneak out! I'll be free!

Dominique and Arwen are in front; they're not

looking. Shalini's behind; she probably won't tell on me. I whisper to Jess, "Cover me. I'm escaping." I head for freedom. I have one foot on the grass when Jess drags me back by one arm and Shalini drags me back by the other.

"You can't escape that way," says Jess. "That's the Toadspit garden."

Shalini looks scared to death. "Ophelia. You must never go in the garden without a teacher," she says. "It's incredibly dangerous!"

I give them a frown from *The Book of Frowns For Fed-up Faces*. "But I saw the Toadspit garden from the dormitory. It was small and this is huge!"

"It can be whatever size the witchwood wants," says Shalini. "Like the cauldrons." She pulls me away to where Dominique's standing at a table, waiting. I don't think she saw my escape attempt. There are seven rows of tables. Seven rows of seven. Our table's sticky, dusty and a bit lopsided. There's one chair at the top and three on each side. The chair legs are thin and the wood is rough. The girls touch

the table and chant.

"Witchwood, witchwood, do the deed, change to be what I now need."

The table straightens; a damp cloth appears and wipes away the dust and sticky marks. It sets itself with cutlery, place mats and crystal glasses. The chairs look sturdier, comfier, smoother. Safer to sit on. We sit. I touch the table and whisper, "Witchwood, witchwood, hear my plea. Send me home in time for tea." Nothing happens.

Girls arrive and the hall comes alive with colour and noise. Stained-glass pictures appear in the windows and doors. Trees, plants, cats, sunshine and storms. The colours shine on the flagstones, shifting and

changing like a kaleidoscope. Ms Toadspit whizzes in and out, strangling girls and pulling up socks.

Witchwood roots are slowly growing in from the garden, surrounding the windows and crawling across the walls. Witchwood kittens are leaping about, chasing each other through the roots. They're connected to the tree by their tails as if they're ac-chew-ally growing from the witchwood, like flowers. They're all quite different but one stands out because its left eye is bigger than its right, and its right ear is bigger than its left. It's cute.

A mouse, a real one, scurries into the dining hall and the kitten pounces. Its tail comes free from the roots with a CRACK and a SNAP! It chases the mouse under the tables and chairs until it escapes through a hole in the skirting board.

Dominique sees me watching. "It should not have missed," she says. "Mice are a blight on the witchwood."

The kitten loses interest and wanders between the tables. It rubs up against my leg and sings a meow. It's a little bit like the flutey sound I heard earlier from the garden. It jumps on to my lap and curls up as if it belongs there. It feels warm and cosy.

I stroke its big ear to a point. It's almost twice the size of its small ear. "I think I'll name you Oddbod," I say.

No one responds. I look up. They're all staring at me and the kitten.

"What?" I say.

"That never happens either," says Jess. "Witchwood cats don't like being stroked."

"Well," I say, giving Oddbod a tickle on his tummy, "that has to be more proof that I am not a witch. More proof that I am a normal person."

Dominique is about to speak but she's distracted by something behind me. Is there food coming? I swivel round. There is no food. She's looking at the boards. They're flashing, dividing into columns. Names. Ticks in Year. Ticks Last Week. Ticks Yesterday.

Comments. The columns fill up.

Arwen is at the bottom of the red board. **Dominique** is at the top. Ticks earned in year: 4975. Last week: 149. Yesterday: 21. Comments: Outstanding witch with a strong desire to succeed.

I can believe that.

"I have earned the most ticks so far this year," she says. "Far more than any other first year."

"You've been here longer than any other first year," says Jess.

Jess's name is at the bottom of the green board. Ticks earned in year: 1006. Last week: 60. Yesterday: 5. Comments: Must conform and comply to succeed.

That sounds sad.

Shalini isn't paying attention to the boards. She only has 998 ticks for the year, but she's new so that's good. And she earned 140 last week and 19 yesterday, which is nearly as many as Dominique.

The smallest board now has THE BEST AND BRIGHTEST WITCH OF THE DAY written across the top in red letters. Dominique's picture appears in the frame. She smiles. "I have been the Best and Brightest every day since I arrived nine months ago," she says.

I ignore her. I cannot believe they put your report on the wall for everyone to see. It's appalling. Another name appears under Jess's on the green board.

Twinkle (?), Ticks earned in year: 0. Last week: 0. Yesterday: 0. Comments: Unknown potential.

"Who's Twinkle?" says Jess, looking around. "What's potential?"

I say nothing as Shalini answers quietly, "It means the other new girl, Twinkle, is full of possibilities and no one knows who she really is yet. Or what she can do. But I wonder why Ophelia's name isn't up yet?"

I continue to say nothing.

Shalini takes a piece of paper out of her pocket, unfolds it and slides it across to me. "Look, Ophelia, this is why you must never go into the garden."

At the top it says *The Toadspit Times*, Y1 School Magazine. Editor, Arwen of Aberystwyth. There's a picture of a scary-looking beetle with big teeth. The headline underneath says: *Beware the Beasties! This week: The Scarabites!* Shalini reads it upside down.

"Scarabites are nasty little beetles that come out at night. They're bright red and make a bitey sound like teeth chattering. They live in tunnels and swarm across the ground if their nest is disturbed. They can eat a cow right down to the bones in five seconds so if you see them, run! Or you'll be as dead as a dead thing that's no longer alive." She whispers the last bit.

Arwen nods. "It's true. You should read Ms Splott's book, *The Beasts and Plants of Toadspit Towers*. It has pictures. Scary pictures."

"I'm saving up for it," says Shalini. "It's good to know what's out there. Best to be prepared." She tucks the paper back in her pocket.

Oh, dungpats. That garden is a nightmare and I still have no way out.

**Summary:**

*Great Escape Plan A: The Find a Map and Secretly Leave Plan. Opportunities – zero.*

★

*Great Escape Plan B: The Great Stink Bomb Plan. Smell level – low.*

★

*Great Escape Plan C: (formerly D) The Have Some Sort of Very Small, Tiny, Non-life-threatening Medical Crisis That Would Require an Ambulance Plan. I am still saving this as a last resort. In case I get it wrong and it becomes a MAJOR medical emergency.*

★

*Great Escape Plan D: Kill the Tree. I like the tree. I shall remove this plan.*

*Great Escape Plan Z: The Climb-over-the-Roof plan.*
*This is my second last resort.*

★

My stomach rumbles. There is no food. Where is the food?

Ms Sage arrives followed by Ms Thorn. Ms Sage is still wearing her bunny slippers but she's changed into a long blue dress with swirls of yellow sequins that match her hat. Horatio is on her shoulder; his owly eyes are fixed on me again. Ms Thorn is dressed the same. Fangus is on the front of her hat like a big black brooch.

Ms Sage coughs. The girls stand. I don't. Dominique *tsks* in annoyance.

"Good morning, girls," says Ms Sage.

"Good morning, Ms Sage," says the girls. I don't.

She bows her head. "Here are the Seven Unbreakable Rules of Ms Ursula Toadspit." Another board appears, behind Ms Sage. Ms Toadspit whizzes across and perches on top. Rule one appears. Ms Sage says it like a prayer.

"Rule one. Only the seventh girl child may enter Toadspit Towers because the seventh girl child is a special child."

The girls answer. "Ms Toadspit rules. We will obey." I don't.

The next rule appears. "Rule two. Students will be given rewards for hard work and attainment."

"Ms Toadspit rules. We will obey."

"Rule three. Students will not engage in frivolous activities."

I wonder what frivolous means. I'm suspecting it's another word for fun.

"Rule four. Students must be neat and tidy."

The girls chant. I don't. Even though Dominique is now glaring at me.

"Rule five," says Ms Sage. "Students will not run in the corridors."

I did this. More proof I'm a normal. Although I wasn't technically a pupil at the time.

"Rule six. Students will not leave the dormitory at night."

"Ms Toadspit rules. We will obey."

"Rule seven. Only students who complete the graduation challenge will have the honour of calling themselves Witches of Toadspit."

"Ms Toadspit rules. We will obey."

"These are the Seven Unbreakable Rules of Ms Ursula Toadspit, Headmistress of Toadspit Towers. Deceased."

They all say deceased like deeee-ceased, and sit down. Ms Toadspit spins into a tornado and whooshes out into the garden, leaving a trail of emerald sparks.

Ms Sage lifts her head and peers over the top of her glasses at the girls. She holds her hands at her heart as if she's in danger of fainting with delight. "My dears. Today we welcome a new pupil to Toadspit Towers."

She's looking at me. Oh, dungpats. I look down. She keeps talking.

"Although her witch hat is concealed and her family tree is currently unknown, the familiars of Toadspit Towers are in agreement." Horatio fluffs his feathers and Fangus shows his fangs. "Twinkle is, without doubt, a witch. Step forward, dear," she says, holding her hand out to me.

"Twinkle?" exclaims Dominique, frowning.

"Ophelia?" says Jess. She's squinting at my head, puzzled.

The rest of the girls are craning their necks to get a look at the new girl too.

"Come along, dear," says Ms Sage in her sweetest voice. "No need to be shy. Up you come." She's smiling her smile of certainty. She's expecting me to comply. Just like last night. How does she make what she wants seem so reasonable? I suspect magic.

I hesitate, just to show her who's really in charge. Then I step on to the stage and it does seem like the sensible thing to do as I do it, and I feel silly for not having done it straight away. I shake the feeling off as I look at the girls. The younger ones are at the front. The older behind.

I suddenly realise Ms Sage has given me an opportunity to explain to the whole school that I've been kidnapped. I take centre stage and bow. I shall give them a speech they will never forget.

"Gentle girls, lend me your ears and hear my tale of woe. Make haste and save me from the tyrant Sage and her lackey, Ms Thorn. For I am held against my will. By some mischance, they have declared me a witch. But I am not Twinkle. I am Ophelia. I am an actress. I have a very important performance in two sleeps." I correct myself. "ONE sleep! So I beseech you, help me escape from Toadspit Towers today."

I think the girls believe me. They're whispering to

each other. Ms Sage is smiling. Ms Thorn is not.

I keep going. "Tis my destiny to appear in William Shakespeare's *A Midsummer Night's Dream*. I must wear a donkey's head and perform my Bottom."

There's silence. Then laughter. Loud falling-on-the-floor laughter.

I attempt to explain, shouting over the noise. "Bottom is a man. He's been turned into a donkey by Puck, the mischievous fairy! Well, not all of him. Just his head."

That makes them laugh even more. I'm getting a bit cross.

"The play will be a tragedy if I'm not there to perform my Bottom! It's a very big and important part!"

A girl in the third row is having hysterics. It wasn't that funny.

Ms Sage puts her arm around my shoulder. "Very entertaining, dear," she says. She waits for the girls to be quiet. She raises her hand. They shush.

"Now," she continues, "I realise that you can't see

Twinkle's hat but it shall be revealed in due course as soon as Twinkle accepts her witch name." She pauses, as if she's giving me time to say the name of ridiculousness. I don't. She gives up and turns to Ms Thorn. "Twinkle will need her equipment, Constance."

Ms Thorn dangles a charm bracelet from her pointy red fingertips. There's a book, a copper cauldron and a tiny wooden spoon clipped on. She flicks it towards me and it fastens itself loosely around my wrist. I feel like I've been handcuffed to the school.

"Off you go," says Ms Sage. "I'm sure you must be hungry. I know I am."

I am and, for once, I'm glad to be off a stage. That really did not go well. I fiddle with the bracelet but can't find a catch.

Jess is looking at me, confused.

"I'm not lying," I tell her. "I am Ophelia." Which is of course technically a lie. "I have no witchy hat. Ms Sage is wrong."

"Ms Sage is never wrong," says Dominique,

squinting at my head. Arwen is frowning with concentration but I can tell she can't see a witchy hat either. Neither can Shalini.

"Well, she's wrong today," I insist. "Granny found me. In a basket. Under a bush. Exactly like I told you."

"Under a bush?" says Jess, like a detective who's just had a clue. She hasn't heard the Granny Wart story. "In a basket?" She considers me for a moment. "You don't know who your mam and dad are?"

"I do not."

"So," she says, looking me straight in the eye. "You actually *could* be a witch."

**10**

"Well…" I don't like the way she's thinking. She's supposed to be on my side. "No! Absolutely not! There is no hat of witchiness." I pull my woolly hat down and fasten the traily bits underneath as if that is proof.

Jess nods in that wise way she has. "Ah. The missing hat of proof." She glances past me and her face falls. "Uh-oh, breakfast's here. Ms Brewbody's looking a bit frazzled."

A harassed-looking witch with a yellow hat and yellow hair sticking out at all angles is leading a procession of large floating trays full of plates and bowls. She flicks her spoon and, one at a time, the dishes glide off to settle in front of the girls. Some look disappointed but others dive in hungrily.

Our tray arrives. A bowl of chopped banana and pineapple and a pot of strawberry yoghurt lands in front of Dominique. Arwen has the same.

Hurrah for witchy breakfast. Bananas are my favourite fruit and pineapples are my second-favourite fruit. I can leave the yoghurt. Why on earth did Jess groan?

A bowl lands in front of me. This is not yoghurt. This is not fruit. "This is not food," I declare. "This is … GLOOP!" I wrinkle my nose up as the smell hits.

"That's an excellent name for it," says Jess as she lets the lumpy, sludgy mess fall off her spoon back into her bowl. "I call it Toadspit Stodge." She closes her eyes and swallows a whole spoonful. "It reminds me of my mam's porridge."

I think her mam must be the worst cook in the world.

She swallows another spoonful and another. "Always eat the bad, then the good," she says, as a slice of hot buttered toast lands in front of her. "You can have half of my toast if you like."

I politely refuse. "I can't take your toast, Jess." I really want to.

She cuts her toast in half and waves a piece under my nose. "You can. You will. You must comply," she says.

I give in and take it. It tastes delicious. I eat the good and leave the bad.

Shalini pauses with a spoon of gloop at her lips. She's also doing bad then good. "Perhaps you'll be able to earn some food in transformation," she says. "We have Ms Thorn after breakfast."

*Oh, joy*, I'm thinking.

Dominique laughs but it isn't a nice laugh. "Honestly, Shalini. How can Oooooopheeelia the actress earn food if she is not a witch? She will have to eat GLOOP," she does air quotes, "every day until she proves to Ms Sage that she should be allowed to leave."

Great giant pats of dung! What a thought! I have to get out of here today or I will starve!

**11**

**Summary:**

*Great Escape Plan A: No escape route noted from any corridor on the way to Ms Thorn's classroom after breakfast. No maps found.*

★

*Great Escape Plan B: I considered smearing gloop on my clothes because it smells disgusting but I don't – because it smells disgusting and I may faint.*

★

*Great Escape Plan C: Still considering what sort of injury would be small enough not to hurt but big enough to need an ambulance. Could I act a heart attack?*

★

Ms Thorn's classroom is a gloomy room of dullness.

Even though they all respect the witchwood at the door it doesn't brighten. I don't touch the witchwood because it made me happy and I'm too annoyed to want to be happy. There's one arched window into the Toadspit garden. It's closed. I'm too warm.

Large wooden plaques are screwed to the stone walls. *Creativity Creates Chaos. Uniformity and Conformity Activates Ability. Imagination Conflicts and Confuses. Conform. Comply. Perfect. Succeed.*

More girls join us. They all have first-year cat ties but their hats are all sorts of colours. They're looking at me. Then looking away when I look at them. I act normal. Because I am normal. Dominique and Arwen dash to the front to sit with two other red hats. Jess sits at the back and Shalini sits next to her. I get the last seat, on the other side of Jess.

There's a book on every desk. *An Instructional Guide to the Proper Poetry of Transformation* by Ms Constance Thorn. It opens at page 35 of 1752. Transformation 15: Slugs to Butterflies.

Ms Thorn arrives. Fangus swoops around the

classroom. Girls duck. He hovers in front of me staring at me with his beady little eyes. I stare back. The girls go quiet. Ms Thorn is waiting. She taps her fingernails on the desk and Fangus flies to her wrist and immediately turns into a charm.

"Good morning, witches," says Ms Thorn.

"Good morning, Ms Thorn," the girls reply. I don't.

There's a copper bowl on Ms Thorn's desk. "Attend, observe and learn," she says. She takes a

slug from the bowl, places it on the palm of her hand and points a wooden spoon at it. She blinks once and the slug is immediately transformed. One nano it's a slug, the next it's a plain ruby-red butterfly that matches her hat. Despite myself, I am impressed.

We watch it flutter to the closed window. It's trapped.

"You will earn two ticks for each successful transformation," she says. "You will only use the poetry spell in the book. You will be examined on these standardised rhymes during your yearly challenge. Any witch using her own rhymes will have ticks removed, not added."

The bowl floats through the air and each girl takes a slug. Not me. My stomach rumbles. It rumbles again. I rub it. I have to have more food soon or I will die. But how do I get it? Idea! New *Great Escape Plan D: Annoy the teachers by asking lots of questions! Then they'll demand I leave.*

I put my hand up.

"Ms."

"Yes, Twinkle," says Ms Thorn.

I correct her. "Ophelia. How do I get better food?"

"You earn it," says Ms Thorn.

I put my hand up.

"Ms."

"Yes, Twinkle."

"Ophelia. How do I earn it?"

"With ticks," says Ms Thorn. She looks around the room. Everyone has a slug. They're all holding wooden spoons. "Eyes closed, girls. Step one. Clear your minds." She closes her eyes and makes a noise like *Hmmmmmmmmmmmmmm*. "Enter your zen space. The empty space in your mind. The space of peace and harmony."

I put my hand up.

"Ms."

Ms Thorn pauses for a moment before opening her eyes. "Yes, Twinkle." There's a hint of a hiss to the yes. Plan D, annoy the teacher, is working.

"Ophelia. What do I get the ticks for?"

"For succeeding, of course."

She closes her eyes again. *Hmmmmmmmmmm*. "Step two, see the spaces, move the atoms, visualise the slug changing to the butterfly. Step three, allow the rhyming spell to form in your mind. From ugly slug to gorgeous bug, a butterfly to please the eye. Step four, channel the power of the witchwood and open your eyes."

Jess opens her eyes. Her slug has shrivelled to a tiny black splodge that looks like hedgehog poo. There's only one butterfly fluttering around the room. Dominique's. It's red, exactly like Ms Thorn's.

"Well done, Dominique," says Ms Thorn. There's a tiny hint of a smile on her lips. "First ticks of the day for the Best and Brightest." She draws two ticks in the air with her spoon. They disappear.

Another butterfly flies. It's bigger than Dominique's, and prettier. It has a pattern of blues and greens, and an edging of golden yellow. It lands on Shalini's finger. She's smiling.

"Plain is best," says Ms Thorn. Shalini's smile disappears. Ms Thorn gives her one tick. Which is just mean.

I flick back through the book to see what they've already transformed. Spiders' webs, dandelion clocks, thistledown, human hair. I'm bored. How can

I earn ticks if I'm not a witch?

There's a green flash. The Toadspit Tornado is spinning outside the window. She materialises on the windowsill and peers into the classroom with her wooden nose pressed against the glass as if she's looking for someone naughty. I hope it isn't me. A few tendrils of hair escape from her bun as she whizzes off again.

Ms Thorn makes me jump. She's at my desk.

"Ms Sage would like you to be tested," she says. "You must comply."

I flinch in case this is some sort of witchy torture but she places a piece of paper on the desk. Stage One: Witches Assessment. It's one of those multiple-choice tests. All about spells and potions. There are boxes to tick. Aha! I'm bound to get some right even by guessing.

"With what shall I tick them?" I ask her. I have no pen or pencil.

"You have your witchwood," says Ms Thorn, pointing to the miniature wooden spoon hanging from my wrist. She turns away and walks back to her desk.

"Just unhook it," says Jess. "Like this." She shows me how. "It can be whatever you need. Just say, 'Witchwood, witchwood, do the deed, change to be what I now need.'" Her spoon changes to a butterfly. She sighs and changes it back.

I say it. The spoon changes. It feels tingly, like the witchwood doorframe. A sharp pencil point appears on the thin end. This transformation does not mean I am a witch. Granny has lots of witchy gadgets. They always work for me too.

The first question is: Which of the following is the key ingredient in a calming potion? Answer: Nettle Roots. Nettle Leaves. Nettle Stings.

Granny uses stings. I have one tick! I shall not starve!

Second question: Which of the following is the key ingredient in an Expanding Potion? Toad Spit. Toad Slime. Toad Tears.

I have no idea. I tick Toad Spit. The tick disappears

and I wonder if the pencilspoon uses disappearing ink. But then a tick suddenly appears in the box for Toad Slime. Which is weird.

Question three: What are the three main attributes of a Toadspit witch? There are ten to choose from. Healing. Status. Warts. Caring. Power. Loving. Cackling. Riches. Sharing. Cleverness. Sneakiness.

I think of Granny and tick Healing, Caring and Sharing. The ticks move to Cleverness, Status and Power.

Someone or something is moving my ticks!

I nudge Jess out of her zen space. "Look at this,"
I say. "The ticks move." I show her. She nudges
Shalini. I show her too. They're both doing looks
from *The Book of Puzzlement.*

Ms Thorn coughs. "You may not ask anyone for the
answers, Twinkle. Toadspit witches do not cheat."

I wonder whether to tell her it's ac-chew-ally the
paper or the pencilspoon that's cheating but I don't
because I need ticks. Ticks mean pies. Or pizza. Or
pasties. So I keep ticking and the ticks keep moving. I
have no idea whether the answers are right or wrong.
I put my hand up.

"Ms."

"Yes, Twinkle."

"Ophelia. I'm finished." I wave the paper at her.

Ms Thorn looks surprised. "So soon?" she says as she walks between the rows of desks. Her witchwood leg is taking big steps towards me and it's making her lopsided. She whacks it with her walking stick with a thump of annoyance. The girls turn to look at me as she goes past. She picks up the paper. She marks. I can't see whether she's ticking or crossing. She stops and raises one eyebrow. Really high. The other one goes down at the same time. It's an interesting look. I store it. I call it *the curious eyebrow look*. I await my results.

"It appears you have earned twenty ticks," says Ms Thorn. I can't tell whether she's pleased or not. "They will be added to your account and you will receive a catalogue." She goes back to her desk.

Twenty ticks! I will not starve! I will have FOOD!

Dominique whizzes round and glares at me. "You got them *all* right?" she says. Now she's doing the curious eyebrow look too. I shrug.

A catalogue appears on my desk. *Toadspit Treats*. It's full of the BEST STUFF IN THE UNIVERSE!

There are sections on food, clothing, books, herbs, artefacts, and one very interesting one called *Customise your Cauldron* with drawers, posters, cushions, cuddly toys, etc. There's a couple of pages on bedding. *A comfy mattress, custom-made to fit your cauldron – thirty ticks. A deep-filled duvet – twenty ticks. Year group duvet cover, cats, bats, snakes, etc. – ten ticks.*

If I *was* a witch I'd be in witchity heaven. My tummy rumbles when I scan the food section. Toast, one tick. Sausage, two ticks. Egg, two ticks. Fruit pie, four ticks. Cake, just like Dominique's huge chocolate cake, ten whole ticks. My mouth is watering for a fruit pie. I need sugar for energy. I may have to climb over the roof after all.

"Just touch what you want with your witchwood," says Jess. Then she closes her eyes and another slug shrivels.

I comply. I order three pies, one for each of us. Which leaves eight ticks. I continue flicking. Then DISASTER! I spot the thing I should have spent the

ticks on. A book. *A History of Toadspit Towers* by Ms
Athena Sage, which has a fold-out map of the school
at the back. A map TO FREEDOM!

But it costs twenty ticks. And I only have eight. I
need more ticks.

I put my hand up. "Ms."

Ms Thorn ignores me.

"Ms."

She still ignores me.

"Ms."

She continues to ignore me. I know I can win but I get sidetracked by Jess. She's shushing me. There's six shrivelled slugs on her desk.

"I need to concentrate," she says, "and you're in my zen space. If I don't make a butterfly I'll have gloop for supper."

I shush and fiddle impatiently with my pencilspoon while she has another go. She points her spoon at a live slug and closes her eyes. She whispers the instructions. "Enter the zen space."

I wonder if I have one. I close my eyes and try to look inside my head for an empty space. I see nothing.

Jess whispers, "Visualise the butterfly."

*Butterflies should be colourful*, I think. *Like big flying rainbows.*

Jess whispers, "Allow the rhyming spell to come unbidden."

I can't remember the spell. I make one up. Just for fun. Because I am bored. *Slimy slug to butterfly, like a rainbow in the sky.*

Jess whispers, "Feel the power of the witchwood and …"

The pencilspoon feels warm. My fingers are fizzingling.

"… open your eyes."

I open them. There's a big rainbow butterfly in front of Jess!

Jess looks startled. "Whoa! I did not see that in my zen space! Why is it so big? And why isn't it yellow? It should be yellow."

I say nothing. I am shocked. It's the butterfly I saw.

Jess nudges Shalini and whispers, "Shalini, did you make me a butterfly?"

Shalini shakes her head. "It wasn't me." She sees my face, which is still doing a look from *The Book of Still Shocked*. "I think it was Ophelia."

"I think it was," I whisper.

Then Jess says the worst thing she could say to me.

13

"So you are a witch!" says Jess. "I knew it!"

I jump as Ms Thorn drops a pile of papers on my desk. "Ms Sage wishes you to continue being tested until you begin to fail. You will comply."

She can't help but see the giant butterfly on Jess's desk. "You have obviously used an unapproved rhyme, Jessica," she says. She waves her spoon and the butterfly turns back into a slug. "Refer to the book and try again. Two ticks removed."

That's not fair! Jess starts to protest.

"But, Ms Thorn," she splutters. "It was—"

I think she's about to say it was me not her so I kick her under the table and interrupt.

"It was my fault," I say. "I distracted her out of her zen place."

Ms Thorn still draws minus two ticks in the air even though I've taken the blame. "It seems you are a disruptive influence, Twinkle," she says.

"Ophelia," I correct her.

She points her spoon into the corner by the window and a desk grows out of the floor. "You may sit over there to finish your assessments. Off you go."

She waits while I move. I comply so I don't get Jess into more trouble. I sit down and put the pencilspoon on top of the papers. I don't think I should touch it. But if I don't touch it I can't tick. And if I don't tick I can't get the book. And if I don't get the book I can't get the map. And if I don't get the map I can't escape. And if I don't escape people will never see my Bottom.

I pick it up. It tingles. I tick. I don't even read the questions. I tick any box and the ticks move. One test, two tests, three tests. I keep going until the last paper has been ticked. I take them to the teacher.

Ms Thorn marks them straight away. Her curious eyebrow becomes curiouser and curiouser until,

finally, she checks the last one and neatens the papers into a pile. She studies me, squints at my head for a moment and then announces, "You have conformed and complied and succeeded. You have one hundred and fifty ticks."

A hundred and fifty ticks! Surely she'll realise that I couldn't possibly have got that many without magical help. Even a Best and Brightest like Dominique couldn't get that many!

"You may return to your original seat," she says. She opens a window behind her. "This lesson is almost over, girls. You may release your butterflies into the garden."

Dominique glares me a glare from *The Book of Glary Glares* as I go back to my seat. I don't care. I'm witchy rich. I can get the book! I can escape!

The room is all a-flutter with butterflies now. Shalini has a plain green butterfly sitting on her finger, one hanging from each ear and three on her head.

"Yay!" cries Jess. "Just in time." She has a

beautiful golden butterfly on her thumb and a pile of dead slugs on the desk. "I can have chips!"

I quickly flick to the book pages in the Toadspit catalogue. I touch the picture of the book with my pencilspoon. A speech bubble appears in the air. It says, *You are not allowed to buy this book. By Order of Ms Sage.*

A bell rings. The catalogue disappears.

Oh, dungpats!

**14**

**Summary:**

*Great Escape Plan A: The Find a Map and Secretly Leave Plan. FAILED!*

★

*Great Escape Plan B: The Great Stink Bomb Plan. There has been no opportunity to increase the smell factor. Perhaps I should jump up and down.*

★

*Great Escape Plan C: The Have Some Sort of Very Small, Tiny, Non-life-threatening Medical Crisis That Would Require an Ambulance Plan. I will not attempt to injure myself until after dinner. I like pies.*

★

*Great Escape Plan D: The Annoy the Teachers by Asking Lots of Questions Plan. This seems to be working quite well.*

★

Ms Thorn orders us out of her classroom. Dominique and Arwen send scowls my way as they disappear down the corridor. They're so cross they forget to drag Shalini with them.

Shalini doesn't seem to mind. As soon as they've gone around the corner she turns to me. So does Jess. Their eyes are twinkling with excitement.

Jess blurts out, "You have to be a witch! That butterfly was amazing!"

"Maybe you are, Ophelia," says Shalini.

This sort of wrong thinking must be stopped at once. "No." I say it firmly, with one hand up like a lollipop lady halting the traffic. "I am definitely, positively, absolutely not a witch. There's only one explanation for this." I hold up the pencilspoon. "This pencilspoon is magic."

They glance at each other as if I'm mad.

"Of course it's magic," says Jess. "It's witchwood."

I shake my head so hard my pompom wobbles.

"I know that. I mean it's been enchanted. To do whatever it can do to make me think I'm a witch." I don't think they believe me. I explain. "That's why the ticks moved. That's why the slug changed."

"But who would enchant your spoon?" says Shalini.

"I have no idea. But it doesn't matter. I know I'm not a witch because—"

"You would feel it in your elbows," says Jess.

"Exactly. And I don't."

A bell rings.

"We have to go," says Shalini. "Ms Lobelia will be waiting and we don't want to lose ticks for being late." The corridor is dark so they light up their hats and I follow. I tell them about my failure to buy *The History of Toadspit Towers* in the hope that one of them owns the book and the map to freedom but they don't.

"Ms Sage will have a copy in her office," says Jess. "She has a copy of every book in there."

"But why did she stop Ophelia buying it?" says

Shalini.

"So she can't escape?" says Jess.

I nod. "That makes sense. She might even be the one who enchanted the spoon! To make me think I'm a witch! That makes even more sense."

"But why does she want a normal to think she's a witch?" says Shalini.

I don't answer because I don't know.

Ms Lobelia's room is big and bright even before we pay our respects to the witchwood. I touch it because I don't mind being happy now. Jess has to pull me off. There are French doors open to the world at the front of the room. I have a moment of excitement until the plants turn their leaves in our direction and I realise it's the Toadspit garden again.

The desks are arranged in an arc. There are three seats left at one end so we take them. We're facing Dominique and Arwen. They're still practising their scowls.

"Welcome, welcome, welcome!" booms Ms Lobelia. She ac-chew-ally has the boomiest voice in the world and the chubbiest chocolatey cheeks. She's wearing big brown boots, baggy trousers, tied round the ankles with string, and a jacket of many pockets. Tendrils of curly brown hair are escaping from underneath her lime-green hat that is covered in velvet ivy leaves.

There's a creature on her shoulder. Like a rabbit with a squirrel's tail. It has big silver whiskers, shiny black eyes and a big black nose. It's sniffing Ms Lobelia's top pocket. She taps his nose. "Treats later, Sniffler," she says.

She unhooks her spoon and waves it about

as if she's testing it.

"Hurrah," says Jess. "It's singing. I love singing."

She is bonkers. This lesson is obviously nothing to do with singing. This is definitely gardening. There's a plant in a pot on each desk. They look a bit like the Venus flytrap that Mr Marlow brought in last term. The flytrap has things that look like teeth. When flies land it traps them. But really, they have to be pretty stupid flies to get caught because the trap shuts really slowly and they can easily fly away if they want to. The plants on the desks are much faster. They're snapping like baby crocodiles.

Ms Lobelia beams at us. "You have in front of you a vernicious veraptor. One of the most dangerous plants at Toadspit Towers. Until you master this plant you must NEVER enter the garden."

I put my hand up and say, "Ms, I have absolutely NO plans to enter the garden of death."

"Ah, the new girl!" She says it with an even bigger smile. "How sensible, Twinkle." I think she's going to be difficult to annoy. "Of course, if you do ever happen to accidentally end up in the garden the trick is to stay on the paths and don't touch anything you can't control. And, most important of all, remain silent. Especially at night."

She waves her arms. The little finger on her left hand is made of witchwood. She's obviously made a mistake at some point. "Ready, girls. Let's sing!" She walks around the room flinging her arms wide, using her witchwood spoon to conduct us. Sniffler has climbed on top of her hat and he's conducting too.

"Up, up, up, everyone! Warm up those voices. La, la, la, la, laaaaaaa. Come along. Doh, doh, doh, doh, doooooooooh. Me, me, me, me, me, meeeeeeeeeee."

So it is about singing. The girls follow Ms Lobelia around the room, copying the notes as they swing their arms. Some more enthusiastically than others. Jess is one of the enthusiastic ones. She whirls her arms around like windmills and sings her heart out. Completely out of tune.

Dominique and Arwen are copying every

movement the teacher makes, like a game of follow the leader. I'm not sure if Shalini's singing. She might just be mouthing the sounds. I do not get up. I do not sing.

"And sit," says Ms Lobelia after a particularly long "Raaaaaaaaaaaaaaaaaaay."

They all sit. I remain sitting because, as previously mentioned, I had not stood up.

Ms Lobelia puts her hands on her hips and grins. Sniffler copies, showing two big white teeth.

"Lovely," says the teacher. "That's got the brain cells working! Now. Listen carefully, or you could lose a finger." She wiggles her witchwood finger at us. "Your task today is to send a vernicious veraptor to sleep." She indicates the plant on her desk. "As this is your first attempt I'm not expecting miracles. I shall award two ticks to any girl who succeeds in making their plant drowsy or droopy. In the unlikely event that anyone sends their plant to sleep I shall award five whole ticks! Woo hoo! Here we go."

She bends down and sings softly to the plant. Like

you would sing to a baby. The plant stops snapping and shuts its trap. It droops until it's flat out on the table. If plants could snore, this one would be doing it. I feel sleepy too.

"There we are, girls," she whispers. "Your turn. Unhook, and channel the witchwood!"

The girls comply. I don't. I have enough ticks. Plus I can't sing. The room fills with noise.

Jess is singing. "Row, row, row your boat, gently down the stream." She's bouncing to the rhythm. So is the plant.

Shalini is leaning in close to her plant. She's whisper-singing. I can't hear her, I can just see her mouth moving. Her plant is already droopy.

Dominique is not singing. She has her hand up.

"Yes, Dominique?" says Ms Lobelia.

"Surely we should all be singing the same song, Ms Lobelia."

"Oh no, that would never do," says Ms Lobelia briskly. "Not in this lesson. Lullabies, girls, lullabies. The aim is to send the vernicious veraptor to sleep.

We're not at a disco."

Dominique does not look pleased. I sit back. I shall daydream of escape until dinnertime. I look through the window. The Toadspit Tornado's whizzing through the plants, sucking up the dead leaves into a giant leaf ball. She spins it up into the sky and it disappears into the clouds. She gathers another. Does she ever sit still?

Jess jabs me in the ribs. "Ophelia, your plant! You'd better start singing before it eats you."

My plant's moving but not in the right way, which would be away from me. It's pushing itself towards me with its leaves, dragging the plant pot behind it. I put my hand up.

"Ms! The veraptor thingy is attacking me!"

"Sing, child, sing!" sings Ms Lobelia.

Well, that's not helpful. The vernicious veraptor comes closer. *Snap, snap, snap*. I don't know any lullabies. I try the latest Messy May song. "*Whoa, what ya singing? You singing that about me? Boy. Whoa, what ya saying? You saying that about me?*

*No?"*

It doesn't like it.

I try a Dzay. *"Yo dude. What up with you. What's with the frown? Don't you know the man's in town? Yo dude. No dude? Yo dude!"*

The vernicious veraptor obviously has no musical taste. It's snapping as if the notes are flying from my lips and it's catching them. I lean my chair back on its back legs. It jerks me forward again towards the plant. *Snap, snap, snappity-snap!*

"You must soothe the beast, Twinkle," sings Ms Lobelia. "Use your spoon. Let your true voice come forth."

I unhook the spoon. I need a weapon. I grip the handle and aim it. My fingers fizzingle again. I open my mouth to say *keep back* and suddenly I'm singing. But it's not my voice. I know what my voice sounds like and this one is not mine. This one's musical. Like a flute. A ghostly flute.

15

I grip my spoon tighter. The fizzingle fizzes up my arm and into my throat like a burst of tiny bubbles. The voice that is not my voice goes up and down. "Ta dee dum dee dee dum dee dee dum dee dee. Ta dee dum dee dee dum dee dummee dee." I close my mouth. It stops. I open my mouth. It starts! I'm like a loudspeaker on an old-fashioned record player.

The enchanted spoon has ac-chew-ally enchanted me!

"Oh man, you can sing AND act," says Jess grinning. "That is seriously impressive."

I glare at her. I shake my head in denial and try to say, "This is not me!" I fail.

"Dee dum dee dee dum dee dee diddy dee dee," sings the not-my-voice. One, two, three. One, two, three, goes the spoon. The plant flops. Not just droops. Flops. As if I've sprayed weedkiller.

Ms Lobelia dashes over and envelops me in a squishy hug. "Oh, how marvellous!" she booms. "We have a natural. Five ticks to Twinkle!" She dumps a bigger plant on my desk. "Try this one," she says.

The not-my-voice sings. The plant sleeps.

"And this one," says Ms Lobelia, dragging me over to a veraptor in the corner that's too big for her to lift.

I sing. It sleeps.

Everyone is watching me except Dominique. She's gripping the edges of her desk in annoyance and singing "Baa Baa Black Sheep" through gritted teeth, which can't be easy.

I feel good. This is ac-chew-ally fun! Even though it isn't my voice.

Ms Lobelia drags me towards the garden and booms, "VERNON!"

Ms Toadspit's there, hanging from a spiky twig by one hand. Her hair's escaping her bun and her hat's

wonky. She points at my head. "Still **no hat; now,** why is that?"

I don't answer because Arwen **screams. A** ginormously huge vernicious veraptor is **pushing** its way towards the classroom. It's **far too tall to fit** inside. It has three traps and they're **big enough to** chew legs off, not just fingers. I repeat **my promise** from earlier. I am never, ever going **into that garden.**

"Come along, Twinkle," says Ms Lobelia, beaming. "Don't be afraid of Vernon. He's a pussycat."

He's nothing like a pussycat! I try to say this but the voice is still in charge. It sings. It works. Soon Vernon is ac-chew-ally purring and I'm acting not terrified as Ms Lobelia makes me stroke his hairy leaves.

Ms Toadspit's still there. She's very still. I wonder if I've sent her to sleep too. Suddenly she jerks, as if she's woken from a dream or nightmare, and spins off in a hurry.

Ms Lobelia turns me round to face the class. "Twenty ticks to my twinkling superstar!" she announces.

Dominique leaps up. "But you said five was the top mark, Ms Lobelia."

"Indeed I did," said Ms Lobelia. "For one. What Twinkle has achieved is outstanding." The bell rings for the end of lesson.

"It wasn't me," I whisper to Jess and Shalini. "It was the pencilspoon." I've hooked it back on to my bracelet. They nod as if they agree.

Dominique is glowering and glaring. I really must see if there's a book called *The Book of 50 Ways to SMILE NICELY* in the catalogue. It could be my leaving gift.

Ms Lobelia gives out ticks for everyone as they queue up to leave the room. "Five for Shalini," she says. "Five for Arwen. One for Jessica and one for Dominique for trying."

Dominique can't believe it. "One?" She squeaks the number at Ms Lobelia. "But I was distracted by Twinkle's singing. We really should all sing the same song! To make it fair."

She slams a chair out of the way. It slides back, tucking itself neatly under the desk. She marches to the door. Arwen trails after her. "I couldn't help getting five ticks, Dominique," she whispers. "I'm Welsh, you see. We can all sing."

I'm starving but I don't want to follow Dominique and Arwen. Shalini's helping Ms Lobelia put the plants outside so I join in. So does Jess.

"Thank you, girls," says the teacher. "I shall plant these up with the fourth..." Her voice trails away. Flowers are blooming on the plants, like a film on fast-forward.

"Look at that!" says Ms Lobelia. "How odd. They don't usually have flowers. They must have cross-pollinated. We could have a new species!"

"Ms Lobelia," says Shalini. She's pointing at the witchwood tree in the distance. It looks normal. Dull green and a bit misty.

"What did you see?" says Ms Lobelia.

Shalini frowns. "Well, I thought for a moment the leaves had turned red but I must have been mistaken."

16

Ms Lobelia shoos us out of the classroom saying, "You'll be late for lunch. Off you go."

"That was strange," says Shalini as she lights up her hat. The corridor is dark. "I'm sure it turned red."

I walk away. "Let's talk about it while we eat," I say. I walk faster. Pies are waiting and my stomach is empty. Plus I have to find a way to get the book and the map. "Hurry up. I have a surprise for you." Oddbod appears in the darkness ahead. I run to meet him.

Shalini shouts, "Ophelia. You're running! You can't run!" Her voice is squeaky with surprise.

I almost trip over Oddbod as he weaves in and out of my legs.

Jess catches me up. "You've broken the rule!"

"I know," I say. "I broke it before, when I arrived. It's no big deal."

"It's a huge deal," says Jess. She isn't squeaking like Shalini but she sounds shocked. "No one can run in the corridors. It's impossible. Watch."

She runs. She hesitates and stops. She runs some more.

"I can run!" she says.

Shalini tries it. "Me too!"

They're both doing a look from *The Book of Puzzlement*.

Jess folds her arms. "Hm," she says. "Mysterious happenings are happening. I suspect we are starring in a MYSTERY. *The Mystery of Toadspit Towers and THE NEW GIRL*." She holds her fingers up one at a time. "Let's examine the unusual occurrences. The witchwood high-fives you. Ms Sage thinks you have a hat. Oddbod lets you cuddle him. The ticks go in the right boxes. You sing Vernon the Veraptor to sleep."

"That was not my voice," I say quickly. "It was the

spoon." She nods as if she's adding this evidence to her list. She's used up all her fingers so she moves to the other hand.

"The flowers bloom. The witchwood tree turns red, for a moment. And now you've broken Ms Toadspit's no-running rule."

"And so have we," says Shalini.

"Yes, we have," says Jess. Then she says to me, "But you're not a witch because—"

"I have no hat. I don't feel it in me elbows and Ms Sage has enchanted the spoon to keep me here. I don't know why."

Jess closes her fingers. "I see. So we *must* investigate and work out why—"

I interrupt. "No. We must not. I'm an actress not a detective. I will find a way to get that map. I will escape and there will be no mystery to investigate for I shall be gone."

Oddbod jumps into my arms and meows. I don't think he wants me to leave.

17

The dining hall is full when we get there. Oddbod jumps down and joins the other cats in the witchwood. There's lots of meowing and whisker-rubbing. It's like a cat conversation.

There are three pies on our table and a catalogue. I order an extra pie because I've been delayed and I'm starving. I can tell Jess hasn't given up on her detective work. I feel like she's looking at me through a gigantic magnifying glass. She needs a Sherlock Holmes hat.

Dominique and Arwen are already there. Dominique glares at her sandwich, my pies and me. Arwen mutters something about liars under her breath.

As they think I'm a liar, I lie. "I can't help it," I say.

"I can sing. I'm just so talented in so many ways. I'm thinking of going in to musical theatre when I get out of here."

Dominique makes her *tsk* noise. She leans in towards Arwen, blocking the rest of us out. Which is fine by me. Ms Brewbody delivers my extra pie. I hold one out to Jess.

"Jess, my friend, would you like a whole blackberry pie all to yourself?" There's a sticky dribble down the side that looks extremely tasty.

"Oh, wow." Jess is staring at the pie as if it's a gigantic birthday cake. "Really?" She takes it. "Thanks!"

I slide an apple pie across to Shalini. She glances at Dominique, who is still making a point of not noticing any of us. "Thank you," she says quietly.

We all tuck in. Jess and I take big bites. Shalini nibbles.

This is the best cherry pie EVER. Sweet sticky juice dribbles down my chin and I consider letting it drip on to my shirt, which will add to Great Escape

Plan B. But I lick it all up instead. The pies were bigger than I thought and I'm full up with one. I wonder what to do with the spare one.

Arwen's eating her sandwich but Dominique hasn't touched hers. She keeps glancing across at the boards. Wondering if she'll be second? Or third? They haven't changed yet. She's biting her lip. Almost chewing it. That's what I do when I'm trying not to cry.

I suddenly feel sorry for her. I've rocked her world of best witchiness and she's probably never had only one tick before. I wonder how I would feel if an Oscar-winning actress turned up at St Bluebottle's and took all the best parts? In a moment of generosity and sympathy I push my spare pie towards her and Arwen.

"Dominique and Arwen," I say, in the kindest voice I can act. "Would you like to share this cherry pie?"

Arwen's eyes light up but Dominique sneers and says, "We are not hungry." Arwen looks disappointed but says nothing.

Suddenly a bell rings and my pie disappears.

Jess sees my shocked face and grins. "Don't panic, it'll be in your cauldron cupboard," she says. "You can have it for supper."

Ms Sage arrives, followed by Ms Thorn. They're talking quietly as they pass our table. I try to listen.

Ms Sage says, "It could be a sign of something. But what?"

I don't hear Ms Thorn's reply.

A long line of teachers enters the hall. Tall, short, fat, thin, old and creaky teachers with hats of many colours and shapes. It's a hat fashion parade. Some are smooth and silky, like Ms Thorn's, but some are rough and bumpy with feathers and sparkly brooches or bands of ribbons and swirls of lace and sequins.

Those teachers who can't fit on to the stage stand at the sides. The oldest ones magic up witchwood chairs and sit in front. Ms Thorn stands next to Ms Sage. She's the tallest and the youngest.

Ms Sage claps her hands and they all hold out their wrists and unhook one charm each. The hall fills with squawks and squeaks and growls and meows as the charms transform into a zoo of flapping, shaking and preening creatures. They perch, stand and cling to their owners.

Ms Sage claps her hands again and, all at the same time, the teachers and creatures turn and stare.

At me.

The teachers all go cross-eyed. Every one of them. I gulp and sit still. Maybe this is some sort of ritual for every new girl. I whisper to Jess, "Does *this* usually happen?"

She whispers back, "No."

Suddenly the noise starts up again. It's chaotic. The teachers crowd around Ms Sage. They're leaning over her, making her seem smaller than ever. She's nodding. Smiling. Her hat is glistening with golden sparks. Ms Thorn is the only one not smiling. Her face is once again blank of emotional information. Fangus is hanging off her ear. They're both watching me.

Ms Sage claps her hands again and they all shush and step back leaving her at the front. She waits for the pupils to shush too. She holds her hands to her heart.

"Girls," she says seriously. "Something rather unusual has occurred. Something that has never been known before in the history of Toadspit Towers. You must prepare yourself for some extraordinary news."

I hope this has nothing to do with me.

"As we all know, our ability to control spare space is based on the ability of the witches at Toadspit Towers to channel the witchwood. This requires power. The power that comes from the genes passed down from witch mother to witch daughter. Our oldest and most respected teachers, Ms Brambury, Ms Rowanstall and Ms Lovage have held the fabric of our school together for the past fifty years."

Ms Sage claps and everyone joins in. Three teachers get to their feet and take a bow. They're the wrinkliest teachers on the stage. They all have blue hats. I check the boards. Blue is six of seven. None of the pupils are six of seven. That board is empty. So is the white board, seven of seven.

"Unfortunately," says Ms Sage. "Due to their rather advanced age they are tiring and, consequently, the school is crumbling. The West Wing is no longer safe. The grounds are wild and untended. Windows are broken and, as you can see," she waves her arm at the teachers, "we have no other blue hats to take over and we fear for your safety."

I'm hopeful! I wait for her to say: *and so we are closing. You can all go home.* She doesn't.

She switches from serious to cheerful. "Which is why I am absolutely delighted, and so relieved, to announce that my colleagues and I have observed, investigated and concluded that our new pupil, Twinkle, is that rarest of witches. That jewel of the witching world. A witch not seen since the death of Ms Nutmeg in 1742. A seventh of seven! Twinkle has the potential to save the school from destruction!"

Oh, giant pats of dung! She has to be kidding.

The whiteboard clicks. My not-name appears at the top. Dominique can't believe what she's seeing. She ac-chew-ally believes Ms Sage.

Ms Sage will not stop talking. "Twinkle is therefore a witch of great power." She's so excited, she's clapping her hands like a baby seal again. "She has the power to change everything!"

Dungpats and warty boils. Now they'll never let me out!

"Noooooo!" I cry. I'm on my feet and shaking with crossness. "I am *not* a witch. I have no power! I am an ACTRESS!"

"You are a liar," says Dominique. She reaches across and pulls my woolly hat off by the pompom. I try to stop her but … DISASTER!

My hair is revealed. Purple, orange and green spiky hair. With streaks of blue. Granny tested her latest product on me. As a birthday treat. It didn't work. I'd asked for golden curls. There's laughter. The dining hall fills with the sound of scraping chairs and curious voices as they all stand up to get a good look.

I can feel my face going bright red. I grab my hat back from Dominique and pull it down firmly. I hold on to the pompoms. Ms Sage calls for hush.

"However, Twinkle *must* accept her name to

reveal her hat and accept her destiny or the school is doomed," she says. She does her smile of certainty at me.

I do not move. I will not give in. I fold my arms. I grip my elbows. I stare straight ahead. I don't act ignoring everyone. I *am* ignoring everyone.

Ms Sage gives up for now. "Perhaps later," she says. She dismisses the teachers and girls with a clap and a wave.

Dominique and Arwen are first to leave. Dominique bashes into me as she goes past. "You are not special. You are a fraud. You are a fake," she says.

"A phony and a cheat too," says Arwen.

I do not respond.

The hall gradually goes quiet as teachers, creatures and pupils file out. I can feel them staring back at me as they disappear through the double doors. Ms Sage and Ms Thorn are the last to leave. They pause at our table.

"Look after Twinkle, girls," says Ms Sage to Jess and Shalini. "I'm relying on you to keep her safe and secure until she reveals her hat."

Ms Thorn touches her shoulder. "The teachers are waiting for you in the staffroom, Ms Sage. We should go before Ms Liverwort falls asleep."

"Of course," says Ms Sage. "We have much to discuss. It's so exciting! There are so many possibilities! A seventh of seven! Off you go to your Toadspit task, girls. If we look after the school, it will look after us."

I don't move as they leave. I am living in a pit of gloomy doom that stinks of despair. Jess and Shalini wait. I can sense them watching me.

"This is obviously a case of mistaken identity," I say eventually.

They both nod but the nods are wobbly uncertain nods.

"Ms Sage is old and confused," I continue. "So are the others."

They nod more nods.

"If I was a witch I would feel witchy."

More nods.

"I would feel it in—"

"Your elbows," finishes Jess.

I nod. My pit of gloom goes darker.

Jess sits up straight and slaps the table. "Ophelia. There is a way to prove you're not a witch."

I have a glimmer of hope. "How?"

"Say the name," she says.

**19**

*Summary:*

*I am the prisoner of a bunch of mad witches.*

*My acting career is finished.*

*My life is over.*

*I shall die tragically of despair way before my twelfth birthday.*

★

"Twinkle. Twinkle. Twinkle," says Jess. "Just say it. When no hat appears, it'll prove you're not a witch. No hat, no power, no destiny."

Oddbod meows in agreement. The other cats in the witchwood roots look up. They leave their prowling, playing, and snoozing. Jess starts laughing as the cats surround us.

"Look at that," she says. "That never ..." she

pauses as she sees my face, "… happens."

"But what if I say the words and there is a hat?" I say. "What if I'm wrong? What if I was the one making the ticks move? What if I was the one singing after all? I'll be stuck here forever. No one will ever see my Bottom. I'll never win an Oscar. But I can't be a witch. I would know, wouldn't I?"

"I always knew," says Shalini. "Grandma was a soothsayer, she saw my future in the cards. But I've always felt it too. Like a tiny tingle through my bones."

"I didn't," says Jess. "I only found out on my eleventh birthday when I accidentally said Jessica, Jessica, Jessica."

I'm not sure I believe her. "How do you accidentally say Jessica, Jessica, Jessica? No one does that."

"I was pretending to be Grandma. She's always saying it. Like this." She slowly shakes her head and looks disapproving. "Jessica, Jessica, Jessica. Whatever will we do with you?"

Oddbod meows. A clock chimes. Two o'clock.

Should I do it? Should I say it? Should I risk it?

I say, "Twinkle." Nothing happens. I don't feel different. I say it again: "Twinkle." I feel nothing. I'm wondering whether to say it again when Arwen yells.

"TWINKLE!" She's holding the door open. "JESS! SHALINI! Dominique is waiting! Our task will not complete itself!"

I stop. I don't say the third. Why would I risk staying in a school with Dominique and Arwen? I stand up and the cats scatter. Oddbod jumps from my knee to my shoulder. He curls his tail loosely round my neck.

Jess looks disappointed.

"Back to Plan A," I say. "Find a map of the school and secretly leave. I need to break into Ms Sage's library. I need to steal *The History of Toadspit Towers*." I head for the door Arwen has slammed shut. I have no idea where I'm going.

"You'll get caught!" says Shalini.

"Not if we help her," says Jess. They both get up

and run after me.

Shalini squeaks, "But what if we're seen? Ms Sage is bound to find out. Or Ms Thorn. She'll put us on gloop forever!" She's still coming up with *but*s and *what if*s when we arrive in a long corridor. Dominique is waiting impatiently at a cupboard door. Arwen is inside the cupboard holding out broomsticks and bags.

"Shalini, you will collect the catash," says Dominique in a very bossy voice.

Arwen hands Shalini an armful of small canvas bags and a small sweeping brush. I have no idea what catash is. It sounds like a sneeze.

"Jessica." Dominique speaks directly to her, ignoring me. "You must show the liar what to do. You will clean the spiders' webs from—"

Jess interrupts. "Don't make us do the north corridors again, Dominique," she says. "There are always loads of webs to sweep up. It's really not fair."

"But this time there will be three of you," says

Dominique. "So you *will* do the north corridors."

"And that is fair, Jessica," says Arwen. She hands us both a big broomstick and a large canvas bag. They take their equipment and walk away. Or perhaps strut would be a better word. They *strut* away.

Jess grins at me. "Let's go! Ms Sage's library is in the north corridors."

I start to run but Shalini pulls me back. "Don't. Someone might see you."

As predicted, there are lots of cobwebs. A couple of witchwood cats are prowling in search of mice. Oddbod jumps down from my shoulder and rubs whiskers with them.

"We'll have to sweep some up as an alibi," says Jess. "Twizzle your broom like this." She lifts her broom into the air and spins it on the end of her finger. It swirls across the ceiling, catching up the sticky webs like candyfloss on a stick. Then she puts the broom into the bag and it comes out clean.

I try it but I'm an actress not a circus performer and the broom won't stay on my finger. So I sweep them

from the ceiling in the normal way. They drop on to
the floor and I twizzle them there. They're incredibly
sticky. We work our way quickly towards Ms Sage's
library and soon our bags are full of webs. As we pass

the staffroom it sounds like they're having a party.

Every now and then Shalini sweeps up little piles of golden ash. She's very careful to get all of it.

We turn a corner and there's Ms Sage's yellow door. The gargoyle knocker is watching out of the corner of his eye. Jess and Shalini look at me. Jess is nodding. Shalini's biting her lip. Oddbod sits in front of the door and meows at me. I don't think he wants me to go in.

I face the gargoyle. "We're the special spiders' web clean-up squad," I say, holding up the bag and broom. "Ms Sage's orders. We must clean." For a second I think he's going to stop us. Then the door opens.

I enter. Jess enters. Oddbod enters. Shalini steps forward then, she steps back. "I can't," she whispers. "I just can't." She takes another step back. "I'll keep watch." She shuts the door.

20

Poor Shalini! I feel guilty. I shouldn't have let either of them help. I'll find the map fast and get out then they can both get back to normal.

I drop my broomstick by the door. Where to start! There are thousands of books in here. I really didn't think this through. Oddbod leaps on to Ms Sage's desk. There's a pile of books next to him. They almost topple over. *Winnie's Almanac, The Hag's Heritage, The Divas of Toadspit.* The pile on the floor is all about potions. *Hubble Bubble, A Teaspoon of Magic, 50 Ways to Clean Your Cauldron.* Maybe there's a history section, like in a proper library.

"This is impossible, Jess. We'll never find it," I say.

"Oh, yes we will," says Jess. She unhooks her

spoon and closes her eyes. "Witchwood, witchwood, take a peek, find the book that we now seek."

Jess is pulled forward by the witchwood. I follow. It takes us in and out of the tall bookcases, around piles and piles of books. She stops. The spoon points up. Jess drags a ladder along the bookcase. "Up you go," she says.

It's a long way up. As high as four of me. Maybe five. The ladder is creaky. I don't look down as I go up. I find the book. It has a hard leather cover and it's as big as my chest. It's so

heavy I have to balance it on each step as I climb back down. I get to the bottom and I hug it as if I love it. "Let's go," I say.

We race for the door. We pull it open. Shalini looks so pleased to see us but the gargoyle takes one look at the book in my arms and says, "You are not allowed to remove that book. By order of Ms Sage."

"But I have to have this book," I cry as the door slams shut with us still inside.

The book struggles to escape from my hug. "Jess! Help!" It's like trying to hold a squirming cat. The book wins and I'm dragged back through the bookcases. Jess holds on to my shirt, trying to pull me back to the door. We stumble and trip over the piles of books. All the way back to the ladder. I give up and let go. The book zooms up and back on the shelf.

"Now what?" says Jess.

"I have an idea," I say as I put my foot back on the first rung. "Ms Sage doesn't want me to have the book so I don't escape. So I won't take the book. I'll just take the map."

I climb back up the ladder and retrieve the book. It does not resist as I bring it back down. It does not resist as I carry it towards Ms Sage's desk. It does not resist as I open it. It doesn't even resist as I unfold the map. I rip it out of the book with a dramatic flourish. "Ta da!" I say with a grin of success. "Off we go."

We open the door. Shalini hisses, "Hurry up. Ms Liverwort has left the staff meeting!"

I wave the map at her. "It's OK. We have the map!" The gargoyle sees. The door slams shut as he repeats, "You are not allowed that book. Any page at all. By order of Ms Sage."

"Aargh and dungpats!" The page flies out of my fingers and attaches itself back to the book. You can't see the tear. I think fast.

"I have another idea," I say. "I shall memorise a way out. Ms Sage can't stop me taking my brain out of her office."

I open the map out. Once, twice, three times. The school is huge. Oddbod jumps on to the map, getting in the way. I move him off. He jumps back on. I pick him up and hold him.

The map is a maze. "Where are the doors? I need a door!"

Jess taps the map with her witchwood. "Show all doors out of the school," she says. Only one red cross appears. She touches the cross and a hologram appears above the map. It's the door I came in.

"That's no good. It has a gargoyle guard. He'll never let me out. There has to be another way," I say desperately. "A window? A secret tunnel?"

I like the idea of a secret tunnel. Unless it was a really narrow secret tunnel. One that got smaller and smaller as you went along. Until you were trapped. That would be bad. I'll stick to a window. There are lots of windows. A memory tickles my mind. Windows and bats!

"Look," I say quickly. "Touch there." Jess complies. A hologram appears of a crumbly tower. "A bat flew out of this broken window just before Granny knocked on the knocker. All I have to do is get there and follow the bats to FREEDOM!"

"But that's in the West Wing, Ophelia," says Jess quickly. "The West Wing is out of bounds to all pupils."

"Well, luckily I am not ac-chew-ally a proper pupil," I say.

Shalini pokes her head around the door. "Ms Brewbody has left the meeting. And Ms Lobelia. Hurry up!" She looks terrified. She closes the door.

I trace an escape route from the dormitory to the tower. "Left, right, left, left, right, left, right, right, left, right, up and out." I do it three times, making up a memory story. I close the book. "Job done."

"You can't have memorised it that fast," says Jess.

"Of course I can. I'm an actress. I learn lines. Let's go."

Shalini flings the door open again. "Ms Sage is coming!" she hisses. "And Ms Thorn!"

"But what about the book!" says Jess. "We have to put it back or she'll know we've been in here."

I have another idea.

21

I grab the book and run. When we get to the door the book flies out of my hands and zooms back to the bookshelf.

"Clever!" says Jess, grabbing our broomsticks. We almost fall out of the door as Oddbod scoots past my legs. The gargoyle grunts. The door shuts.

Jess twizzles her broomstick. "Quick. Look busy."

I sweep as Ms Sage and Ms Thorn come round the corner. I don't look at them until they are right in front of us. My heart is thumping. I'm sure they'll hear it. I keep repeating my memory map, hoping it will calm me.

"How industrious, girls," says Ms Sage. "I don't think I've ever seen this corridor cleaner! It's a good beginning, Twinkle." She counts Shalini's bags. "Five bags of catash. The witchwood will be pleased."

Shalini's hands are trembling. Ms Thorn notices. She does the curious eyebrow as Ms Sage says, "I shall reward you with a slice of gingerbread each." She ticks the air. "Enjoy your treat. Run along."

I don't hesitate. I run. Two steps. Jess and Shalini tug on my sleeves.

"Walk," whispers Jess.

Shalini grips my arm like a vice.

I look back as we turn the corner. Ms Thorn has gone in. However, Ms Sage is staring at me. A smile spreads across her face as I disappear around the corner. I suspect it turns into a massive grin.

Shalini whispers, "Did she see? Did Ms Sage see you run?"

"I think so. Maybe. I hope not."

"She'll think it's even more evidence that you're special," says Jess. "All the ticks, the singing, the invisible hat and now rule-breaking." She's sounding overexcited. I'm suspecting that she agrees with Ms

Sage. I'm suspecting she's thought I was a witch all along. Since she heard about the baby in the basket.

I stop us. This is a hands-on-hips moment. I put them there.

"Jess. Do you ac-chew-ally think I'm a witch?"

She hesitates as if she's searching for exactly the right words. "I think you're an actress," she says.

Not exactly the best answer but I accept it. I turn to Shalini.

"Shalini. Do you think I am a witch?"

She too hesitates before answering. "I think you would know if you were," she says. "I think you would feel it. Like me. So no, I don't think you're a witch. But I do think someone or something wants to keep you here. I just don't know why they would do that if you're not a witch."

*Neither do I*, I think.

We return the broomsticks and go back to the dining hall. Ms Lobelia is in the garden. She's standing beside a mountain of spiders' webs and a pile of bags. Ms Toadspit's tornado is whizzing through the garden, gathering up more leaves. Bouncing from plant to plant like a pinball ball. There's a group of girls on the other side of the lawn brewing something in their cauldrons. Golden flames are flickering under the copper; it looks pretty.

"What an excellent haul of webs today," booms Ms Lobelia. She spots Shalini's catash bags. "Five cats! How marvellous. I do hope Twitcher has ashed. He does become rather scratchy and tetchy just before he regenerates. He's much nicer as a kitten." She tips each bag carefully into the witchwood roots. The ash melts into the wood. I watch the ash disappearing into the witchwood and I suddenly realise what catash is!

There's a shriek from the garden. A terrified girl dashes towards us; she's expanding rapidly. Ms Lobelia races to meet her crying, "Lei Mai! I said two teaspoons of grueberry juice not growberry juice! Angelica, we need a tomato!"

I confront Shalini. "Shalini!" I am shocked. "Don't tell me you were ac-chew-ally sweeping up dead cats!"

"OK," she says hesitantly. "I won't."

"But you were!"

"Yes. I was," she admits. I feel horrified so my face must look it. "We have to," she says quickly. "Or they can't regenerate. They get old and crumble into ash. Then we collect them up and return them to the witchwood and they're reborn. It's lovely really."

I disagree. I'm frowning to show this.

"They get to be silly kittens over and over and over again," says Jess. "And as long as we collect the ash, they'll live forever." She's smiling, like it's all perfect.

"Unless the tree dies, of course," says Shalini. "Then everything will die. The school. The cats. The garden. Everything."

This does not cheer me up.

"Don't worry about it," says Jess. "It'll be weeks before Oddbod turns to ash. You won't even be here to see it."

Strangely, this does not cheer me up either. We head for our table. The gingerbread is there. I take a bite. Then another. It's gone. And soon I'll be gone too.

"Now that I have the map," I tap my head, "I just have to go back to the dormitory for my bag and I'm leaving." I lick my finger and get the crumbs.

"Ah," says Jess.

"Er," says Shalini.

"What?" says I. "Why does that get an ah and an er?"

"You can't get into the dormitory," says Jess. "Not without Dominique."

Oh, dungpats. "Fine. I'll leave after tea."

"There's silent study after tea," says Shalini. "In hat groups."

"Then I'll leave after that." Silent study sounds so boring.

"Then it's journal time," says Jess. "In year groups. We have to write down everything that happened today."

"Then I'll leave after that," I say.

They look at each other as if they know there's another problem.

"What?"

"Well," says Jess. "Then we do go back to the dormitory but—"

"Rule six," says Shalini. "Students will not leave

the dormitory at night."

They're not thinking clearly. "But I'm not a real Toadspit pupil. I can break the rules because I ran in the corridor."

Shalini grips my arm. It hurts. "But what about the Toadspit Terrors! What about the big claws and the big jaws and the great big goggly eyes!?! How will you see them in the dark? You'll have no witchlight because you're not a witch!"

Honestly, she really needs my help. I shake my head. "I really don't think there are any beasties stalking the school. Dominique and Arwen have made them up to scare you. I'm sure of it. The only beasties in this school are in the garden and I am definitely NOT going out there."

22

The hall is filling up with girls again. It's noisy. They're chattering, reading, practising spells. Books, catalogues and games are spreading across the tables. A group of girls in orange hats are transforming forks to spoons and back again. Another is using her witchwood spoon as a torch, making scary shadows on the wall. Ms Lobelia's voice is bouncing in from the garden; she's singing with some green hats. I ignore anyone looking at me. Then I have an idea because I've been thinking.

"Shalini." I point to the girl making shadows. "I don't need witchlight. I can make a spoontorch."

I unhook my spoon. The fizzingles tingle up my fingers and then I say, "Witchwood, witchwood, hear my plea, please become a torch for me."

A beam of light shines on Shalini's face. Escape Plan A is complete.

Dominique has arrived but hasn't joined us. Thankfully. She's sitting at another table with an audience of reds. They're hanging on her every word. She flings her arms wide and pretends to sing. I hear the word liar. They all turn and look at me. I act not caring.

Ac-chew-ally, I don't act it. I really do not care. Dominique and her silly Best Witch stuff will all be history by morning. She can be the best at whatever she wants to be the best at, once I've gone.

Now they're all singing. I try not to hear the words but can't help it.

"Twinkle, Twinkle's quite bizarre.

Thinks she is a mega star.

'I'm not an owl, a toad or bat,

I am no witch,

I have no hat!'"

They fall about laughing and pretend to throw their hats in the air.

"Ignore them," says Jess.

"I am. They're like the midges on Granny's nettles. Irritating, annoying, but not ac-chew-ally life threatening." I hand out catalogues. "Food's on me," I say. "I shall spend all of my ticks on my very special witchy friends before I leave."

Jess doesn't need persuading. She orders sausage and chips.

I order a chicken roast dinner with Yorkshire puddings and extra gravy.

Shalini opens her catalogue but before she orders she glances at Dominique and Arwen. They're glaring at us again. I lean over and squeeze her hand. "Shalini. Dominique isn't the boss of you. No one is the boss of you."

"That's easy for you to say, Ophelia. You're leaving."

"But I'll still be here," says Jess. "Stop trying to please her. It's an impossible task. Dominique is officially unpleasable. I've been trying to please her for the last five months and I have failed completely." Jess shakes her head as if she's really disappointed.

Shalini smiles. It turns into a grin. "I love the way you take so long to brush your teeth," she says.

"There you are then," I say. "From this moment on. You are no longer a Dominique-pleaser. You are a Shalini-pleaser." I point to the tasty pictures. "So tell me what you want or you could get mustard custard and a bowl of gloop! I'm ordering, I'm ordering!"

Shalini can hardly speak for giggling. "Butter chicken, I'll have butter chicken, please. Thank you." As I order she rummages in her pocket and takes out the bar of chocolate I gave her last night. It's unopened.

"We can share this while we wait," she says. She breaks it into three and gives us each a piece. We take the first bite together as if we're making a friendship pact. I get all warm and fuzzy inside. I'm going to miss these girls.

I flick through my catalogue. "Cauldrons! What do you need?"

Nearly everything, apparently. Their cauldrons must be as bare as mine. I order duvets, mattresses, fluffy pillows and cuddly toys. Jess chooses an orangutan and Shalini chooses a rabbit. I check my account. I have ticks left.

"What about books?"

Shalini chooses Ms Splott's book, *The Beasts and Plants of Toadspit Towers*. Jess decides on *Transformation Tips: Rhymes and Rhythms* by Ms

Devishi Dubashi.

I inspect the contents page. "Now, what has Dominique got that you two haven't got?"

"A big head," says Jess.

We all burst out laughing and don't notice Dominique and Arwen until they are looming over us.

"You are making too much noise," says Dominique.

"What's so funny?" asks Arwen. "Has Winkle – I mean Twinkle – I mean Ophelia told another enormous lie?"

I'm so fed up with their attitude but I act friendly. "Arwen. I never, ever, lie," I say. Which is, obviously, not quite the truth because I did lie a bit earlier on about the singing. Oh, and a little lie about where I came from. I think that's it. It might not be.

**Summary:**

*This has been the longest three hours of MY LIFE!*

✦

*But now I am ac-chew-ally standing at the dormitory door. I am ac-chew-ally going to get my bag. I am ac-chew-ally going to escape!*

✦

*I have perfected the memory map. I have even written it down.*

✦

*Oddbod has disappeared. I haven't seen him since silent study. I think he got bored.*

✦

*Dominique and Arwen have been not speaking to me VERY LOUDLY. They are NOT winding me up. Oh no. Definitely NOT.*

★

Dominique opens the door. "I think I shall call myself Hooooortensia and perform my nose," she says. "After all, a nose by any other name would smell as sweet."

They've been coming up with Bottom-related jokes all the way back from the dining hall. This is the funniest thing she's said and I almost burst out laughing but stop myself just in time and act not hearing. Jess fails. She laughs out loud. "Wow, Dominique, you have a sense of humour!"

Dominique ignores her. She goes in first, followed by Arwen. She's shutting the door as Shalini, Jess and I go through. As if we don't exist.

Arwen joins in with the loud NOT SPEAKING TO ME. "I may perform my ear," she says. Which is not funny at all. "The world must see my ear." Which is just copying. "I shall call myself Daffodil." Which is just a stupid name.

I start to climb my ladder. I can't wait to get in, get

my stuff and get out of here.

"Oh, but," says Dominique, unrolling her cauldron's ladder, "Daffodil is such a boring name. It is sooooo ordinary. I shall call you Jooooliet. I do believe she dies young in one of the plays. It is all so very tragic. It is a tragedy that only an actress such as I can understand."

They both pretend to swoon.

I CANNOT stop myself. I refuse to act NOT HEARING them NOT SPEAKING TO ME any more. I swing round on the ladder and face Dominique.

"What *is* your problem? I'm an actress. I'm not a witch. I'm not the seventh of seven. I'm leaving. You will never see me again. You can be the best of everything because I won't be here to stop you."

"You could not stop I," says Dominique. She laughs, but there is no giggle or chortle in her laugh. There is an absence of smile. "I *am* the Best and Brightest witch. Everyone knows this."

She's sooooo unbelievable and I'm sooooo cross. "The best! You are so not the best. If you were the best you'd be kinder. If you were the best you'd be helping others. If you were the best you'd be sharing. If you were the brightest you'd be lighting the room up with laughter. You'd be making the school a nicer place. You'd be using your powers for good, not evil."

That was probably a bit too far. She isn't exactly evil. She's just horrible. And mean. And nasty. I finish off with a warning.

"You can't be the best at EVERYTHING. No one can. And you'll end up with no friends if you don't change your ways."

I realise I sound just like Granny and I dive into my cauldron before she can respond. I'm quickly followed by Jess and Shalini.

The cauldron stretches as we all drop down on to the thin mattress.

"Ophelia!" Jess is crying with laughing. "That was brilliant! You really put her in her place."

But Shalini's shaking her head. "No. It isn't brilliant at all," she says. "Ophelia's made a huge mistake. She's just made Dominique incredibly cross."

"Good," I say. "I couldn't be happier. Someone had to tell her. I thought you'd stopped being scared of her, Shalini." I sound disappointed and she looks hurt.

"I'm not scared," she says. "Well, maybe a bit, but that's not what I mean. Have you forgotten? You need to get out of the dormitory and Dominique is the only one who can open the door. You can't escape without her help."

Oh, dungpats!

**24**

*Summary:*

*Great Escape Plan A is doomed!*

★

This is a DISASTER! I am way beyond the LAND OF DESPAIR. I've climbed over a MOUNTAIN OF MISTAKES and into the COUNTRY OF DEVASTATION.

"I'm an idiot!" I bang my forehead on the cauldron wall. *Thunk.* "I completely forgot!" *Thunk.* "She'll never let me out, not after what I've just said." *Thunk.* "I'm trapped. I'll have to eat gloop forever!" *Thunk.*

"Of course she'll let you out," says Jess.

"Oh, no, she won't."

"Oh, yes, she will."

"Oh, no, she won't."

"Oh, yes, she will."

I'm in a panto!

"Why will she let Ophelia out?" says Shalini, interrupting the routine.

I do the curious eyebrow look at Jess. So does Shalini.

"Just think about it for a second," she says. She's also doing the curious eyebrow.

We think. We think some more but soon it's obvious to Jess that Shalini and I haven't thought the same thoughts as her. She gives in and tells us.

"Dominique will let you out because she wants to get rid of you. Because she believes that you *are* a witch. Because you earned more ticks today than she earns in a week. Because if you are the seventh of seven…"

I attempt to interrupt with a denial but Jess keeps going.

"…*you* have the potential to be the best *Best and Brightest* ever. So she HAS to get rid of you."

"Of course," says Shalini. She kneels up in

excitement. "Jess is right. Maybe you'll just have to ask for help in the right way. Take a peace offering?"

"Cake," says Jess. "Cake would be a peace offering."

"I have no cake." Then I remember the pies and the fact that one has been delivered to my cauldron. "I have pie!" I locate the cupboard and inside is my pie.

Jess licks her lips.

"Dominique hates cherry pies," says Shalini. "That's why she said no when you offered one earlier."

"She loves chocolate cake," says Jess.

"But I can't buy cake," I remind her. "I've used up all my ticks."

"We have ticks," Jess says with a big grin. "Don't we, Shalini?" She grabs the catalogue.

Shalini jumps, the cauldron swings. "We do! We can order the biggest, chocciest cake there is."

I can't let them do that. "No. You need your ticks for when I've gone. It'll be death by gloop if you spend them." I try to pull the catalogue from them but they hang on until I let go.

Jess opens it at the cake page.

"I'm ordering, I'm ordering," says Shalini, her spoon getting closer and closer to the page.

"Me too, me too," says Jess.

They both touch the cake at the same time. Two seconds later the biggest and best chocolate cake appears in the middle of the mattress. It's big enough for the whole cast of *A Midsummer Night's Dream* to have a large slice each.

"Do you think it will work?" I ask.

"Cake always works," says Jess.

"Along with an apology," says Shalini.

Apology! I really do not want to apologise for telling the truth. But I want to get out. So...

"I can act apologetic," I say. "If I must. If it can't be avoided. But I definitely won't be sorry."

25

**Summary:**

*Great Escape Plan A will only work if I give the best performance of my Shakespearean career so far.*

★

*I'm standing beneath Dominique's cauldron, with the cake.*

★

"Knock, knock," I say.

Shalini and Jess are peeping out of my cauldron.

"Louder," whispers Jess. Shalini raises her hand, palm up, to agree.

"Knock, knock," I repeat, but louder.

"Who's there?" says Dominique.

Oh, I wish she hadn't said that! I take a big breath and act sensible. This takes skill.

"It's Ophelia. I've come to apologise."

There's no answer.

"I have a peace offering of delightfulness," I say.

I might as well be talking to an empty cauldron.

"It's a cake," I say. "A mega cake of chocolateyness with chocolate icing and chocolate sprinkles."

Dominique's head appears. She leans over the edge and eyes the cake. Arwen joins her.

"You are sorry?" says Dominique.

"For being so rude to Dominique?" says Arwen.

"Indeed I am," I say. I hold the cake up. There are tears in my eyes. There is sadness in my face.

I act apologetic.

"Fair Dominique, hear my sorrow. I spoke the words I spoke in temper and they should not have flown from my angry lips and into your delicate ears. Thou did not deserve those words of harshness."

I act honesty.

"So now I come to speak the truth. Thou art the Best Witch. The witch with the power. The power to free me from my prison of gloom. Only you can open the door of despair."

I act pleading.

"Help me now, oh mighty witch. Open the door and free me tonight. Help me to achieve my destiny."

I act persuading.

"Then thou will never have to see me or talk to me ever again. Thy life will become a life of peace and happiness. Thy mind will be a haven of zen – empty and thoughtless."

I suddenly realise that could sound like an insult but she doesn't spot it.

Dominique climbs down. Arwen follows her. They face me. They fold their arms.

"So," says Dominique. "You need I to help for I am the Best and Brightest Witch at Toadspit Towers?"

"Absolutely," I say, with a bucketful of firmness and a giant nod that hurts my neck. I should get an OSCAR for this performance! "Upon my honour, thou art THE WITCH. Thou art THE WONDEROUS WITCH OF WITCHDOM. I do confess my faults and submit myself to your witchy highness's mercy."

She looks like she's considering what to do. She comes to a decision. "You shall have the help of I."

EXCELLENT!

"When all the school is sleeping. At midnight. I shall open the door."

What! Midnight? Why do I have to wait until MIDNIGHT? There won't be any buses at MIDNIGHT. I'll have to sleep under a hedge or in a haystack until the morning and then find a kindly villager who won't turn me in to the witches but will send me on my way back home with a packed lunch. And what are the chances of that happening?

"But, Dominique," Shalini calls out from my cauldron. "What about the Toadspit Terrors? Ophelia isn't a witch. She'll be eaten in the corridors!"

Dominique looks at Shalini and then Arwen. "You must tell Shalini the truth," she says.

"The truth," says Arwen. There's a hint of a question in her reply.

"You must admit the lie," says Dominique. "There are no Toadspit Terrors in the corridors at night. You will be an honest witch."

I knew it.

Arwen hesitates. "It's true," she says. "I just made it all up to scare you, Shalini." She dances her fingernails across the cauldron. It sounds like scuttling. "It was a joke."

*It wasn't a very funny joke*, I think. Shalini's frowning as if she doesn't quite believe her.

Dominique smiles at me. I think she's happy. "Midnight is a good time. Ms Sage must not know you had the help of I. So you must leave when all is quiet and the school is shrouded in the blackest of darkness."

I really don't like the way she said blackest of darkness. Just darkness would have been enough. Or she needn't have mentioned dark at all. She's obviously trying to scare me but she doesn't know I have a witchwood torch. Ha ha!

"Deal," I say. I hand over the cake.

**26**

*Summary:*

*Great Escape Plan A: Nothing can stop me now!*

★

*Shalini and Jess have reluctantly left me so that I can get some sleep. I have not slept. I have eaten my pie.*

★

I rehearse my story map until the school clock strikes twelve. Then I quickly stuff *The Complete Works of William Shakespeare* in my backpack and put my birthday money in the little pocket, ready for the bus fare when I find a bus. I switch on my spoontorch and climb out.

The door is already open. It's dark in the corridor. Dominique is on one side. Arwen's on the other. Jess is at the bottom of my ladder. She's clutching her new rhyme book and there are four multicoloured butterflies fluttering around her head.

I give her a goodbye hug and she whispers, "Are you sure this is a good idea, Ophelia?"

"Yes," I say. I act bravery. "I know exactly where I'm going and I shall be home for breakfast."

I want to say goodbye to Shalini but there's no sign of her and I need to leave. Maybe she's too worried about being stuck with Dominique to say goodbye. I take a step towards the door but Dominique blocks me.

She points at my spoontorch and holds her hand out. "You are a thief. You must give it to I. It belongs to the school."

I don't want to. "But I'll be in the dark," I say. "Out there." I point into the gloom.

"You must hand it over. The bracelet too."

"I can't get it off. I already tried."

She grabs my wrist and touches the bracelet with her witchwood spoon. There's a click and the bracelet falls into the palm of her hand. She drops it into her pocket and holds her hand out for the spoontorch.

I give in. I can't fight her for it. I might lose.

The corridor is sooo dark, even with the light from the dormitory. For a second I think about not going.

I have no torch. I could get lost. I should wait for morning. I haven't even tried *The Have Some Sort of Very Small, Tiny, Non-life-threatening Medical Crisis That Would Require an Ambulance Plan.*

I see the look on Dominique's face. It's the worst look yet because it's saying, "You are a coward. You will not step out of this room. I know this. For I am the Best and Brightest."

I straighten my back, take a deep breath and step forward. Into the darkness. It's cold.

Suddenly Shalini leaps up in her cauldron, waving Ms Splott's *Beasts and Plants* book above her head.

"OPHELIA! STOP!" she yells. "You're not a witch and there really are—"

Dominique shuts the door in my face with a slam.

**Summary:**

*I am alone in the blackest of darkness with Shalini's words ringing in my ears.*

✦

Dungpats! I cannot even see my nose. There's huge amounts of black. Everywhere.

What was Shalini shouting? I'm hoping it was something like, OPHELIA! STOP! There really are … cuddly puppies lurking in the corridors. OPHELIA! STOP! There really are … fluffy bunnies in the dungeons. OPHELIA! STOP! There really are … sleepy sloths in the towers.

My fingers touch the dusty, cobwebby wall. I think bad thoughts about giant spiders. I block them with an image of a cute kitten. Oddbod. I wish he was with me. But he isn't. I swing my backpack on to my back and set off, feeling my way out. I follow the wall with my left hand and start the memory story.

"Once upon a time I was LEFT at witch school."

My words echo through the corridor. I tiptoe in silence, counting the dormitory doors, listening for beasties. I whisper the next bit.

"Which was wrong not RIGHT."

I walk into a wall. I turn right.

"My granny ac-chew-ally LEFT me with a gang of wicked witches! She LEFT me in gloomy doom."

I turn left through the archway and a quick left again. I pause. Listen. Nothing. Except my breathing.

When I get home I'll have STRONG and FORCEFUL words with Granny. I shall demand a cauldron bed to make up for the trauma. And a trip to the theatre. Maybe two. She should use her witchy powers for good. My good.

"I must escape RIGHT away."

I turn right. My fingers feel greasy. I imagine the trail they've left behind me. I keep going with the story and my journey.

"And once I have LEFT the school of doom I shall perform my Bottom."

Pause. Listen. Nothing.

I'm nearly at the West Wing. If there were any Toadspit Terrors I would have seen them by now. Wouldn't I? Dominique and Arwen wouldn't have sent me out to die by Terror, would they? I try not to answer that question.

"RIGHT, here we go, across the tower and into the West Wing."

I drag my fingers along the right-hand wall. There's nothing in the corridor except me and the dark. There's no noise, no scuttling, no big beasties.

"This is the RIGHT way to the window of freedom."

I've crossed the tower. I'm in the OUT OF BOUNDS West Wing. I'm expecting a magical barrier. A gargoyle of guarding. There's nothing. It's just another rule, a rule I can break. The crunchy, crumbly stones on the floorboards make too much noise as I step on them. My toes are hurting from all the tiptoes.

"Soon I will have LEFT all of this nonsense behind me."

Mr Marlow, my drama teacher, will be soooo pleased to see me. Maybe we'll get a write-up in the paper! *Daisy performed a beautiful Bottom.*

"And then my life will be a life of RIGHTness."

I turn right. There's a flash of green. Down the corridor. Ms Toadspit! I step back. I hold my breath. I don't believe it! I'm so close! I only have two moves to go. I will not be fed UP because I will be OUT of here. I can hear bats. Squeak, squeak, squeak. I daren't move.

I wait. I wait some more. I peep. The corridor is dark. She's twizzled her tornado somewhere else. I take a deep breath. I tiptoe to the right. I see moonlight on the stone steps. I feel fresh air. I feel freedom! I dash towards UP and OUT. I leap up the steps to ESCAPE!

URGH! I run straight into the biggest, stickiest

spider's web IN THE WORLD! A spider's web of superglue! It's much worse than the north corridor webs! I struggle. It sticks. Over my mouth. In my ears. Up my nose.

I curse Dominique. This is her fault! If I'd had my torch, I'd have seen it. My arms are stuck. My legs are stuck. Maybe I can bite my way out? Bite is a bad word. I think of others. Chew. Chomp. Gnaw. Nibble. Even nibble sounds scary.

I hear a sound. Dungpats! It's a real sound. It's behind me! Shuffly sounds. Scuttly sounds. Something wicked this way comes and I don't think it's a little beastie. It's definitely a BIG beastie.

The shuffles and the scuttles come nearer and nearer, louder and louder and I know I'm about to be eaten! By a Toadspit Terror!

I'm an idiot! Everything Arwen said about the Toadspit Terrors is true, and her real lie was that they *didn't* exist, and I'm a fool for believing anything either of them said. I'm about to be very DEAD and it will be ALL their fault!

And, I suddenly realise, Ms Sage won't tell Granny I'm dead because she would get into terrible trouble for *allowing* me to be dead. So Granny will spend *years* thinking I'm alive and at witch school and Jess and Shalini will think I'm alive and *escaped*. So no one will ever know what's happened to me. I'll be FORGOTTEN.

Something tickles the back of my neck and I'm surrounded by flickering light. "Found you!" whispers Jess.

I'm going to live! Tears of relief squeeze through the sticky threads on my eyelids.

"The Toadspit Terrors are real!" says Jess. She's panting, like she's been running. "Ms Toadspit made gigantic spiders in 1694 to guard the school from the Witchfinders. They'll eat anything that doesn't have witchlight. Which is you!"

She points her spoon at my face. She closes her eyes and before I can object she chants firmly, "Change, change, changeroo, from sticky web to runny goo."

The web dissolves immediately. I'm free! And covered in gloop from my hair to my toes. "Yeuch!"

Jess turns her spoon into a towel and wipes the gloop away as she talks. "Shalini stood up to Dominique and Arwen. She was amazing. She threatened to tell Ms Sage that they'd lied about the Terrors and put you in terrible danger. Arwen caved in and opened the door for us but Dominique said she knew you weren't in danger, because you are a witch, because Ms Sage said so, and all you had to do was say your name and you wouldn't die. You should have seen her face when we broke the rule and went into the corridor."

Jess steps back. "That's better. So we followed your finger trail through the dust to save you and help you escape. Didn't we, Shalini?" Shalini doesn't answer.

We look around. There is no Shalini.

There's a scream!

Oh, dungpats! I was so close to freedom! So close to stardom! There's another scream.

"Come on!" I head back down the corridor, pulling Jess behind me. "We'll save Shalini. Then I'll escape."

We retrace our steps. Jess's light is like a searchlight, scanning the floor for footprints. I spot some marks down a corridor to the right. We inspect them. Some look like footprints, small ones. Some look like short stabby lines.

"Uh-oh," says Jess.

I think I'm allergic to uh-ohs. Nothing good EVER follows an uh-oh. No one ever says, uh-oh, here's some chocolate. Or uh-oh, you look lovely. Or uh-oh, you've won the lottery.

"Those marks were not made by human feet," says Jess.

We follow them. Another terrified scream screeches up the stairs just ahead of us.

"I think they're eating her!" cries Jess.

We dash down the creaky stairs. Along a wobbly landing. Down even more rickety and risky steps, following the screams. We burst into a hall as big as the dining hall. We skid to a stop. Walls, windows and doors are covered in ancient, crumbly witchwood roots. Dusty marble statues line each side. They're glowing, like a ghostly audience to the real-life drama in the middle of the room.

29

*Summary:*

*Shalini is about to be eaten.*

*I have given up all hope of escape (for now).*

★

Shalini's surrounded by spiders. Not real spiders. More like a child's drawing of spiders come to life. HUGE drawings! Dog-big. But not pug-sized. Not Chihuahua-sized. Boxer-big. Bulldog-big. They're hairy. And leggy. And fangy. And the great big gruesome googly eyes are all goggling in our direction.

Shalini's hat is casting weird green shadows on her

face. She's doing a look from *The Book of TERROR!*
"Look out!" she squeaks. She's pointing behind us.
A spider drops down from the rafters. Cutting off our
escape.

Jess shines her witchlight into the spider's eyes.
It takes a step back. Into the doorway. But another
spider drops. Then another. We're forced towards
Shalini. We huddle together.

"They're not supposed to attack witches!" she
whimpers. "Ms Splott said so! It's in the book!"

"I don't think they've read the book," I whisper.
More spiders are crawling out of the ancient roots,
creeping over the floor, the ceiling, the walls. So
many eyes! So many claws! So many pointy fangs
going *click, click, click.*

Jess aims her light. They stop but not for her. An

enormous spider drops down in front of them. This one is Great Dane-size with eight of the longest hairy legs and eight of the biggest, blackest eyes, cracked, like broken ice in a puddle. Our terrified faces are reflected a thousand times. I name him Scary!

Suddenly the green tornado spins into the hall. It stops above Scary's head showering him with emerald sparks. Ms Toadspit materialises.

"We're saved!" says Shalini. She stops squashing my arm.

Ms Toadspit's hair is a tangled mess with streaks of silvery grey. Her hat wobbles as she puts her hands on her hips and says, "Oh dear, oh dear, this can't be right, some children not asleep at night. You broke my rule! You're not in bed! You're wandering the school instead! Something's happening, something's wrong. The cats have changed their Toadspit song and witchwood leaves can change from green, which never happens! What can it mean?"

I get the feeling she's not really talking to us. The Terrors are creeping forwards.

"Ms Toadspit," I say. I act calm. "We sincerely apologise for being out of bed. We need you to tell the—"

She doesn't listen. "There's such confusion in my head. So you must all go back to bed! I have far too much to do, to bother with the three of you."

She spins away with another flash of emerald sparks. Out of the hall. Gone!

"I can't believe she's left us!" cries Shalini.

Scary scratches his claws across the flagstones. *Scraaaatch. Scraaaatch. Scraaaatch.* He clicks his pincers. *Click, click, click.* Then big and small and short and tall, the other Terrors join in.

Shalini puts her hands over her ears. Jess too. And me.

"There's only one way out of this," shouts Jess, forcing me backwards. "The garden."

"You have to be joking with bells on!" I yell over the scratches and clicks. "We can't go in the garden. Remember what Ms Lobelia said. You are NEVER to enter the garden!"

"We have no choice," cries Shalini. "The book says the spiders won't go into the garden. They're scared of the vernicious veraptors."

"*I'm* scared of the vernicious veraptors!" I yell.

"But you can sing them to sleep," shouts Jess.

"No! I can't," I shout as we take another step. "I can't sing anything to sleep! That was NOT my voice in the classroom! If we go into the garden, we'll all die!"

"If we *don't* go into the garden we'll all die," yells Jess.

The spiders advance.

I hear the *creak* of a door opening behind me. Cold night air rushes in. I smell dampness, rotting leaves and sickly sweet perfume. Jess pushes me out first, then Shalini. She leaps out, slams the door shut and holds it as the spiders press against the glass.

"There we are. Safe!" she says.

"Safe?" My voice squeaks. I look around in the moonlight. The plants make spooky shadows. "We're in the ac-chew-al garden that no one should ever, ever, ever ac-chew-ally go in. We're not safe. We're doomed."

Shalini's crying. Trying to catch her breath. "Ms Toadspit's gone mad! She left us to die. Just for being out of bed!"

"She's not herself," says Jess as she lets go of the door and puts her arm around Shalini. "Did you see her hair? No bun. And her hat? It was frayed. All around the edges. It's like she's falling to pieces."

"But why?" sobs Shalini.

I check on the spiders. They've all sat down as if they're waiting for us to go back in.

"I don't know," says Jess. "Ms Toadspit's been whizzing around like a force-ten tornado since..." They both look at me.

"Don't say it," I say.

They say it.

"Since Ophelia arrived."

"Don't blame me," I say. "Blame Ms Sage for adding my name to the big book of Toadspit. It's obviously messed up the system. I'm a normal in a school for witches. I'm not supposed to be here. Of course Ms Toadspit feels weird. She can sense it's wrong. She wants me out."

"You could be right," says Shalini, drying her tears on her sleeve. "You're a normal and it isn't normal for a pupil to be a normal."

Jess grins. "Normally."

I join in. "So please can I leave and then everything will return to…"

"Normal," we all say together.

"OK. Let's do it," says Jess. "Let's go back to the West Wing and get you out." She unhooks her spoon. "Witchwood, witchwood, I implore, lead us to the West Wing door." The spoon drags her forward. Her hat shines, lighting up the redbrick path.

"Keep to the path and stay absolutely silent," says Shalini, giving me a gentle push. "And don't touch anything. And keep your eyes open for the little beasties."

I move. "And the big ones," I add quietly.

The plants are thick and tangled. They're so tangled

we can hardly see the bricks. They need a gardener. An army of gardeners. We step and dodge and duck our way through branches, stems and leaves as if we're in some sort of game. Touch one and BUZZ, you're out. We press on in silence. It's so quiet that sometimes I think I can hear Shalini's heart beating. It could be mine, though.

The spoon drags Jess left and right so many times I wonder if it's trying to get us lost. I *am* lost. I'm tired. I need a drink. I need to sit down. I need a bath! I duck under a leaf the size of an umbrella. A trickle of icy water drips down the back of my neck.

"Urgh!" I break the rule of silence.

"Shush," whispers Jess loudly, from in front.

"Shush," whispers Shalini quietly, from behind.

I turn to say, "I was shushing," and I don't see Jess stopping. I bump into her. She stumbles. I stand on Shalini's toes.

"Ouch," she says. Then she whispers, "Sorry," and so does Jess.

"SHUSH," I say to both.

Jess points silently at the path ahead. We've reached another crossroads. It's blocked by a fallen tree trunk. The spoon drags left. Off the path.

Shalini taps me on the shoulder. I turn round. "What's wrong?" she mimes.

"It's blocked," I mouth.

Then she looks past me, over my shoulder, and her face changes from curious to puzzled to scared. I whizz round.

There is no Jess.

**Summary:**
*There is no Jess in any direction – forward, back, left or right.*

★

"Jess," I hiss-whisper. "Jessica!"

There's a scream. From above. "Help!" Leaves and twigs land on my head. "Up here! I think I bumped into Vernon!"

Jess is squirming between the jaws of the biggest vernicious veraptor on the planet of witchdom.

"Don't just stand there, Ophelia," she yells at me. "SING!"

"I can't!" I shout back.

"Just try!" she screams back at me.

I try, I honestly do. But what comes out is MY

voice. Not the voice of delightfulness.

"Tar deeedeee, diiiiiiii dummmmyyyyyy traaa dummmmyyyyyy deeeee tarrrr dummmmdeeee do doo dooo doooo dodeedoooooo."

"He's squeezing me tighter," screams Jess. "Sing properly!"

"I am singing properly! This is how I do it!" I attempt to act not panicking but I can't because I *am* panicking. "Yo dude. What's up with you? Row, row, row that boat. What's with the frown? Don't you know the man's in town? Row, row, row your dude, gently down the stream. Whoa, what ya singing?"

"Ow, ow, OW!" screams Jess. She's hitting Vernon with a thick branch. "Stop singing rubbish, Ophelia! You're making him angry."

I shut up and watch Jess struggle in the jaws of death. This is BAD! BAD! INCREDIBLY BAD! This is worse than being dumped at witch school. This is worse than getting stuck in a spider's web. This is worse than— "OW!"

Suddenly there's a stabbing pain in my ankle and

I'm swept up into the jaws of death. I'm dangling upside down by my right leg. My woolly hat falls off. Blood dribbles towards my bottom. My real bottom.

Shalini's down below. All alone. I remember her plant from earlier. She got five ticks! It went to sleep. She can sing! I yell, "Sing something, Shalini!"

The third trap swoops to snap her up. She dodges. It misses. She unhooks her spoon. She sings. I can't hear her. Vernon squeezes my leg. More blood dribbles. "Louder, Shalini, louder!" I yell.

She closes her eyes. Her voice grows and grows until the most relaxing sound fills the garden. It feels like a lullaby but I can't understand the words. She sweeps the notes up and down and around with her spoon as if the music is a bird flying in and out of the leaves and branches. She looks so peaceful. All her screwed-up nervousness has disappeared. Her hat is glowing, like sunlight shining through a leaf. Shalini is a singer like I am an actress!

Vernon loves it. He's swaying and flopping. His hold is loosening. The ground is a long way away. I fall. Jess falls. Luckily, we land in a big pile of dark-brown soft stuff. Unluckily, it is a pile of stinkyness from the stink dimension.

"Oh, yuck." Jess has it all over her face. She wipes her eyes clear. "This is worse than gloop."

I spit a warm squidgy lump out of my mouth. "This is gloop with added yuck," I say with a grimace. "Urgh." I find my hat. The pompoms are sludge bombs. I drop it in disgust. Granny will have to knit another.

"Uh-oh," says Shalini. Her feet are planted firmly on the redbrick. "You've both left the path!"

I hear a noise like teeth chattering. I think it's Jess.

"Why are your teeth chattering?" I ask.

"My teeth aren't chattering," she says. "Your teeth are chattering."

"No, they're not."

The chattering gets louder. It's coming from everywhere, every crack and crevice. Like thousands of pairs of tiny teeth clicking together with the cold. Sharp, tiny teeth.

"It isn't your teeth," yells Shalini. "You're in a pile of scarabite poo! You've landed right in the middle of a scarabite nest! Run!"

Hundreds of beetles the size of my thumb emerge from holes and gaps in the rocks. Their pincers are as big as their bodies. I don't need telling twice. I leap up and run along the path. A limpy run on a bleeding ankle. I don't know which way to go but any way is a good way as long as it is AWAY! I can hear crashing behind me. I think my friends are following me. "I wish I *was* a witch," I shout back to them. I dodge branch after branch after branch. "Then I would get rid of this stupid garden and plant some proper plants! Plants that don't try to kill you. Like cabbages!"

They don't answer.

I keep on limpy running. I'm breathless and my legs are aching but I can still hear the chattering beetles of death and daren't turn around. My lungs are breaking! I have a stitch in both sides!

At last! I see French doors ahead of me. The dining hall! I see my reflection in the glass, racing towards me in the moonlight.

"This way!" I cry as I leap along the path. "We've made it!" I drag the door open and almost fall over the threshold. It's dark. I turn round, ready to slam it shut once they come through.

But there's no one there. No Jess. No Shalini. Just the scarabites flowing along the path like a beetley river of ruby redness and gory death.

**Summary:**

*I am alone.*

★

I slam the door. The scarabites crash into the glass. Wave after wave of Shalini's little beasties pile over each other like pebbles on a beach. Where are my friends! I peer into the garden through the dead roots that surround the doorway. They're not there.

Suddenly I AM IN A WORLD OF PAIN.

"OW!!!!" I hold my hand up. My thumb has gone! Blood is bleeding! Two scarabites drop off my elbow. They crawl across the stone floor, dragging my thumb with them!

I jump up and down on them. They crunch. Tears of pain dribble down my cheeks and blood drips from the stump of my thumb. Then I think a bad thought. *There could be more! In my hair, up my trouser leg, down my back.* I shake and scream and jiggle and squirm until I'm sure there are no beastly beetles lurking.

I am living in a world of SHOCK! I take a deep breath and wrap my bleeding hand in my tie. I feel faint. I want Granny. I want my friends. I press my forehead against the cool glass. The scarabite eyes flash ruby red on the other side.

Something moves behind me. I turn. I freeze. I act not panicking. This is not easy. This is extremely difficult because this hall is *not* the dining hall. This hall is the assembly hall and I am back where I started. Oh, dungpats of doom. This is bad.

There's an enormous hairy lump curled up on the floor. It twitches, like a dog having a nightmare. It lifts its head. Opens its eyes. It's Scary! The Toadspit Terrors crawl out of the shadows, out of the roots. They drop down from the rafters.

I press my back against the door. The scarabites

tap on the glass behind me. I'm trapped. I'm not starring in *The Mystery of Toadspit Towers and THE NEW GIRL* I am ac-chew-ally starring in *The Tragic Tale of the New Girl WHO DIES!*

I jump as Ms Toadspit streaks through the double doors. She's a doll, not a tornado. Her hair is totally grey now. Her hat's unravelling from the pointy bit. There's a long green thread trailing behind her.

"There you are! You are to blame! The girl who does not say her name. The school feels wrong, the school feels strange and *you're* the only thing to change."

Her eyes glow brighter than emeralds in firelight. The tarnished tree charm around her neck has grown a tiny red leaf.

"So who are you to break my rule? Ophelia, Daisy, Twinkle? Who? Tell me now and tell me true, or it will be the worse for you!"

The spiders click their pointy fangs in agreement. Scary scratches the flagstones. *Scraaatch. Scraaatch. Scraaatch.*

Ms Toadspit raises her hand. The spiders freeze.

I gulp down my fear. "I'm Daisy Wart!"

"Oh, no, no, no, that isn't true, I can feel that isn't you. One name down and two to go, tell me now, for I must know!"

Ms Toadspit's tree charm is spinning. Her hair and dress are blowing in the wind but there is no wind. There's no point left on the hat. Just a brim.

The Terrors creep forward inch by inch. I see myself in a thousand glittering eyes. She doesn't stop them.

"Ophelia!" I cry. "I'm Ophelia, the actress!" My head is buzzing. I feel dizzy. My hand is hurting. Blood is seeping through my tie, dripping on to the cold flagstones. "Help me! Save me from the Terrors!"

Ms Toadspit shakes her wooden head and says, "I cannot help, I made the rule, that Terrors must protect the school from those who are not magic. I fear that if you don't comply, your ending will be tragic. There is but only one name left, and Sage believes that is correct but, even if that name is true, you must tell me, Twinkle who?"

A thread falls across her eyes. She pulls it, gathering up the loose threads into a ball. She drops on to Scary's head. "My hat unravels? Why is that?" She points at me. "It's all your fault! Reveal your hat!"

Scary creeps closer and closer. He smells of dust and mould. He reaches forward with a long leg that ends in a sharp and pointy point. He taps my toe.

My heart thumps. Ms Toadspit is ac-chew-ally going to let me die if I don't say the name! I am living in a NIGHTMARE! And no one is waking me up!

I need help. I need witchwood. I grip the nearest root. Maybe I can have a spoon! If I beg.

"Witchwood, witchwood, I do plead, give to me the help I need! I know you like me, I don't know why, but I need you now or I could die!"

Something leaps from the old roots. The spiders scatter. Oddbod! He meows loudly. Other cats join him. They're purring the flutey song. They are my not-voice!

The witchwood between my fingers fizzingles. Strands of gold flicker through the cold dead wood. It feels warmer. Alive. The floor under my bottom shifts. The flagstones crack. Roots break through. They're thin, as thin as Ms Toadspit's unravelling threads. They weave and twist, and loop over my hand, up my arm and completely cover my body. I'm encased in witchwood armour!

Ms Sage, Jess and Shalini burst into the hall as Ms Toadspit screams in frustration, "Tell me true! Who are you? Tell me true! Who are you?"

The threads reach the missing thumb. They push the tie away. They spin and weave the shape of a thumb. They join it to a witchwood root. I'm like a witchwood kitten, growing from the tree. I feel warm. I feel safe. I feel like Granny's hugging me. A "kiss you better" hug. My toes wiggle a happy dance. I love the witchwood and the witchwood loves me.

Ms Toadspit's stopped screaming. I think she's

crying. But the doll shows no tears. Her hat's almost gone. There's a mass of green threads hanging off her shoulders like a shawl. She sounds desperate as she whispers, "Tell me true. Who are you? Tell me true. Who are you?" She's gripping her charm as if she'll never let it go. She's staring at me.

I stare. She stares. I stare. She stares. This isn't fair. She has no eyelids. I blink and get to my feet. The witchwood armour is like a second skin. It moves with me. I'd be like a witchwood superhero except my skirt is bunched up and I feel like I'm wearing a nappy. Scary takes a step back. Ms Toadspit leans forward. "Tell me true, who are you?" she whispers. She sounds like she's begging now. She floats down on to my hand.

The witchwood threads immediately bind my thumb to the tiny wooden body. Suddenly Ms Toadspit's thoughts and memories foam and froth into my mind, like bubbles popping and bursting in my brain. I know her and she knows me and the witchwood knows everything. It only takes a moment.

"There you are!" whispers Ms Toadspit. "I see you." She sighs and the doll relaxes against my hand. "There you are at last." The light in her emerald eyes fades away.

I am. I'm there. I mean here. And I'm doing a look from *The Book of Shocked, Surprised and Stupefied*! Ms Toadspit has gone from the doll. She's left. Departed. And I know my name. My ac-chew-al real name. I am experiencing an uh-oh moment of emotional mayhem. A monumental and momentous moment of emotional mayhem.

Jess interrupts it with a shout. "Ophelia, are you all right?" Ms Sage is holding them both back.

I am not. I am living in the land of SERIOUSLY SHOCKED!

"I'm not Ophelia," I say, which I knew. "And I'm not Daisy Wart." Which I also knew because Granny is not my real granny. I think I'm delaying because I can't believe I'm about to admit what I'm about to admit.

213

"I'm Twinkle Toadspit. The seventh of all those sevens just like Ms Sage said. And I think I've just killed Ms Toadspit. I think I've just broken the curse."

The witchwood binding Ms Toadspit to my thumb crumbles to dust and I'm holding a lifeless doll. There's a tiny click and the silver charm bracelet falls from her neck. It flicks on to my wrist and fastens. The silver shines brightly and the tree lights up with jewelled leaves. I look at it and can't believe it's there.

"Now they'll definitely never let me out," I say.

32

My witchwood armour falls away, back into the cracks, as Jess and Shalini run over. Oddbod meows and the last of the spiders scatter and retreat into the shadows. Including Scary. The cats stay.

Ms Sage waits for a second, as if she's taking a deep breath, and then follows the girls with a big smile on her face. I can tell that I'm much better than a box of chocolates now. I'm more like a lifetime's supply of chocolate truffles.

Jess is squealing. "Twinkle TOADSPIT! Twinkle TOADSPIT!" She gives me a giant hug. "That's awesome!"

"I don't believe it!" squeaks Shalini, hugging me next. "You weren't a witch, you didn't feel like a witch and now—"

"You're the witchiest witch of all!" says Jess. She's bubbling with excitement. "And you're not DEAD! Does this mean you own Toadspit Towers? Are you the headmistress now? Can I be your deputy? Do you get to make the rules? Are you in charge? Can you make a rule – no more gloop? Can you give Dominique detention!"

Headmistress? Who would want to be a headmistress! Although, giving Dominique a detention sounds good.

Then Jess gasps in horror. "But what if the curse has passed to you! What if you can never leave Toadspit Towers! You'll be trapped!"

That is definitely not going to happen. I start to explain it was just Ms Toadspit's curse but Ms Sage interrupts.

"So many questions, Jessica. I think you'll find making any assumptions as to Twinkle's status in the school may lead to misconceptions and misunderstandings that, of course, can lead to mistakes and misfortune. I think you'll find that as

Deputy Headmistress I shall step forward to fill Ms Toadspit's shoes." She turns to me, leaving Jess to think about what she's said.

"Well, Twinkle dear. I knew you were special but not even Horatio suspected you were descended from Ms Toadspit. This changes everything. With the Toadspit curse broken, rules can be changed and Toadspit Towers shall be saved! We shall become the Biggest and Best witch school once again. How exciting!" The bunny ears are flipping up and down on her slippers. "We must plan for the future!"

Yes. That's exactly what we must do. We must come up with a plan. So far I have *PLAN: ?*

Ms Sage is doing her happy clapping but then she looks at my head and frowns, as if she's only just noticed it's bare of woolly hat and spiky of hair. She stops clapping.

"Oh, dear me," she says. "That won't do. We can't have Ms Toadspit's heir looking like a multicoloured coconut." I flinch as she flicks her spoon at my head. I think she's trying to make my hat reveal itself but she isn't. Her spoon whooshes with a blast of warm air, like a hairdryer on MAX. It keeps blowing until my hair grows to its normal shape and colour. Bramble-bush brown. I am me again.

"That's better," she says. "Now all you need is your hat," she adds. She waits for me to say the name three times. I don't. I'm planning.

Ms Sage gives up and unhooks Horatio. "Please invite Ms Urtica Wart to join us," she instructs him. He flies off into the school as she says to me, "We obviously must involve your granny in the discussion of this unique situation."

"Obviously," I agree, still planning.

Jess is jumping up and down singing, "Twinkle Toadspit owns the school, which is great cos she's no fool." Shalini's giggling.

"You really *must* calm down, Jessica dear." Ms Sage says it with her special smile.

Jess calms down.

"Follow me," says Ms Sage. "I do think hot chocolate and ginger cake for breakfast will be just the thing to celebrate while we await the arrival of Ms Wart. Then we must wake the school and share the amazing news with the staff and girls."

That sounds good. I need chocolate. Chocolate is good for thinking. Good for planning.

Oddbod jumps on to my shoulder and we set off but I forget I'm attached to the witchwood by my thumb. There's a SNAP and it breaks from the roots, just like a kitten's tail. I hold it up. It doesn't hurt.

"Ophel— Twinkle!" exclaims Shalini. "You have a witchwood thumb! You have to be a witch now."

I let them inspect it as we follow Ms Sage to her library. I continue to think and plan. The thinking I am thinking is this:

*What do I do now?*

The plan I'm planning is this:

*The Final Plan: There is no plan.*

We've had two hot chocolates and three slices of gingerbread each by the time Granny arrives. She's come by broom. Much faster than taxis. Horatio has told her the whole story, as much as he knows.

"Well," says Granny, dropping her cloak on the back of Ms Sage's comfy chair. "Ms Twinkle Toadspit? That's a turn-up for the spellbook! So me elbows was right! You is the real deal. You is special. Go on then, show us your hat."

They all wait. They all look at my head. I ignore them. I'm still planning. Still thinking.

*A: I know I'm a witch. I feels it in me bones, especially in my thumb.*

*B: I'm still an actress and I feel that in everything!*

*C: I'm not ready to reveal my hat.*

*D: I'm not ready to give up on my Bottom.*

*E: So I need to ... to ... to...*

I jump up and shout. "I have it! I have a plan!"

**Summary:**

*We're in the dining hall. The teachers, creatures and girls are there, in their pyjamas and nighties (not the creatures). I'm on the stage with Ms Sage and Granny. Ms Thorn is at the side holding a velvet cushion with Ms Toadspit's doll lying on it. Her hair's back in its bun, tied up with a green silky ribbon, and she's been spruced up with a new dress and hat. Ms Sage is waiting to speak. That's it.*

★

We wait as the last few girls stagger in, still half asleep. Dominique and Arwen are right at the back, as far away from the stage as they can possibly be. Maybe they feel guilty for nearly killing me. But maybe not.

Oddbod is sitting on my foot. He keeps tickling my leg with his whiskers. I'm acting patient. Eventually Ms Sage steps forward. She speaks quietly. Seriously. Everyone listens seriously too. The hall is lit by candles, making it quite spooky.

"Teachers, creatures and girls. I have called this early morning assembly because I have some surprising news. The wicked curse that bound Ms Ursula Toadspit to the school of Toadspit Towers has been ..." she pauses for dramatic effect. I'm beginning to think she's a bit of an actress herself, "... broken. Our esteemed headmistress is now officially ... dead."

Ms Thorn ac-chew-ally looks sad as she slowly tilts the cushion forward, so everyone can see Ms Toadspit's doll lying on the white velvet. There's a flurry of shocked chattering.

The chattering stops as Ms Sage continues. "Which means that, after over three hundred years of service, Ms Toadspit can now take her rightful place as the *first* headmistress of Toadspit Towers."

Ms Sage twizzles her spoon on the end of her little finger. A cloud of golden sparkles appear under Ms Toadspit, lifting her off the cushion. She spins over the heads of the crowd, like an extremely slow-motion tornado, across the hall to the doll display.

Her name card disappears and she settles into its place. Her name appears on a shiny brass plaque on the edge of the shelf as Ms Sage says quietly, "I give thanks to Ms Ursula Toadspit, Founder of the School."

Everyone says it. Even me. Even Granny.

Ms Sage waits a moment out of respect. I act patient. She waits another moment. I act even more patient. She clears her throat, then smiles a huge smile before she speaks in her normal isn't-everything-jolly voice.

"As some of you know, the Toadspit curse could only be broken by a very special witch indeed and I'm sure you can *all* guess who *that* is!" She's laughing now. Dominique isn't. Arwen isn't. "The curse could only be broken by …" She is really loving her pauses. It's annoying. "… another Toadspit!"

"Nooo!" cries Dominique, jumping up. Arwen pulls her down as Ms Sage holds out her hand to me.

"And here she is! Twinkle Toadspit. The great-great—"

This is going to take ages! I interrupt. I step forward. I perform.

"Gentle girls and Toadspit teachers and creatures. Tis true." I hold up my Toadspit bracelet; the tree is sparkling with jewelled leaves. "I am Twinkle Toadspit. Breaker of the curse. And heir to the witchwood." I hold up my thumb.

The doors to the garden swing open and the witchwood tree is revealed like a picture in a frame. It's no longer green. It's a kaleidoscope of colour changing with the breeze. Cats meander in and mingle with the audience.

Dominique is now ramrod straight. She's looking

straight ahead as if she sees a future of mess and complications. Arwen has her hand on her shoulder but she's gawping at me. It's an interesting look. Several other people are using it. I continue. It's time for *The Final Plan: Deal A*.

I use my best Shakespearean words. I need the practice.

"Yester morrow, as you may recall, I wouldst not bow to Ms Sage's will. I wouldst not accept my witchdom. I wouldst not accept my fate. And so, at dead of night, into the jaws of the blackest darkness I stepped. Into the corridors of doom I crept. My intention – escape."

This is going rather well. I don't look at Jess and Shalini in the front row. I suspect they're giggling.

"Truly, fate and fortune were not my friends in the gloom of Toadspit Towers. Dear witches, I almost died! Not once! Not twice! But more than thrice!" I consider a pause but now is not the time for pauses. "But I was saved! For two of the Best and Brightest witches risked all to save me from dangerous danger and perilous peril!"

The boards light up. Jess and Shalini's faces appear in the golden Best and Brightest frame. Jess is grinning. Shalini's alternating between extreme embarrassment and happiness, with the occasional glance at Dominique, who is still sitting ramrod straight.

"And forsooth, the benevolent Ms Sage has agreed to award them one hundred ticks each!"

Ms Sage leans forward, "Twinkle dear, that's not quite what we—"

Granny starts the clapping. I clap the loudest and I keep clapping until the ticks have been added and Granny pokes me to stop.

Now for the second part of *The Final Plan: Deal A.*

"I was brought unto this school two days hence by my granny, Urtica Wart." Granny waves at everyone. Some wave back. "To become a witch. To reveal my hat. So here it is. The moment Ms Sage has been waiting for."

I'm a bit reluctant. Doing it in front of everyone is slightly embarrassing. But a deal is a deal. This is a hands-on-hips moment, so I put them there. I take a deep breath.

"My name is …"

I can't help doing the pauses. They expect the pauses.

"… Twinkle Toadspit …"

They like the anticipation.

"… Twinkle Toadspit …"

It makes it more exciting.

"… Twinkle Toadspit!"

My head fizzingles with the biggest fizzingle of all! Suddenly I'm surrounded by disco lights! Red and yellow and pink and green, purple and orange and blue. Something is spinning, whirling and whooshing around my head. I am splashing out a tornado of colour across the hall. My mind feels warm and tingly and excited! Then the spinning slows. Slower and slower. It stops. I feel dizzy. Granny steadies me.

"Twinkle, look," shouts Shalini. She's turned her

spoon into a mirror. She holds it up.

My hat is AWESOME! It's a swirly, whirly hat of rainbow brightness. I LOVE IT! My hat is me. I am my hat! I'm living in the land of SERIOUSLY HAPPY! If I'd known I would feel like this, I'd have said my name ages ago!

Ms Sage is clapping her sea lion clap. And dancing a happy dance. Ms Thorn is standing very still. She's folded her arms as if she senses trouble in the future. As if she knows the words comply and conform are in danger of being removed from the Toadspit dictionary. Dominique has ac-chew-ally fainted. Arwen's fanning her with this week's copy of *The Toadspit Times*.

There's just one last thing to do while I'm on stage. I must reveal *The Final Plan: Deal B Part 1*.

I bow to my audience.

"Gentle girls, lend me your ears and hear my tale of happiness and joy! It has been agreed by Ms Sage that I shall perform in *A Midsummer Night's Dream* this very night at St Bluebottle's Primary School."

Jess and Shalini shout, "Hurrah!"

"And," I continue because I haven't finished, "Ms Sage has kindly given permission for everyone to attend!" I wave my arm with a flourish. "You *must* all come and see my Bottom!"

34

**Summary:**

*The play was an outstanding success! Almost everyone came, and Jess and Shalini declared my Bottom to be incredible!*

★

*We have returned to Toadspit Towers and I am currently lying on my thin mattress under my shabby blanket wishing I was better at negotiating deals.*

★

*These were the deals*

*Deal A: I'll reveal my hat if Jess and Shalini are awarded 50 (ac-chew-ally 100) ticks each and get to be Best and Brightest for a week.*

★

*Deal B: I'll save the school if I get to do my play.*

*The bad news is I forgot to give myself some ticks.*

*The good news is I now have not one, not two, but three plans for saving the school quickly so that I can continue my theatrical path towards stardom and Oscars.*

★

*I try the first. It's genius. I grip my spoon and say firmly, "Witchwood, witchwood, hear my plea. Save the Toadspit school for me."*

★

*Nothing happens.*

★

*Dungpats.*

# Acknowledgements

No witches were harmed in the making of this book. That's mainly down to my brilliant agent, Amber Caraveo, and Kirsty Stansfield, my fabulous editor at Nosy Crow, who was so patient with me throughout the editing process. Thank you. And thank you to Kate Wilson and the whole Nosy Crow team for being so enthusiastic about Daisy. You are all winkling … tinkling … twinkling stars.

There were no witches or spells involved in the long run-up to publication but there were quite a few fairy godmothers:

The Society of Children's Book Writers and Illustrators dynamo, Candy Gourlay, for her constant enthusiasm, encouragement and friendship. Natascha Biebow, Sara Grant, Sara O'Connor, Working Partners and the entire team of Undiscovered Voices volunteers. You made me think I could do this. Chitra Soundra and Elaine Cline for the Slushpile challenge that led to Amber Caraveo discovering and loving Daisy's voice. My lovely NE SCBWI friends who have critiqued and laughed at my work. The first writer I ever met – Christina Banach. We have travelled a rocky road together and the journey isn't over yet. The entire scoobie group: if you've ever commented, encouraged or in any way supported my work, and me, thank you. It's awesome belonging to such a great community.

Candy Gourlay again! For setting up the blog Notes From the Slushpile and letting me be part of the slushie gang. You are all amazingly talented people. Go, slushies! My funeverse poets. You've given me a reason to write silly stuff and a means to share it with the world on the funeverse poetry blog. I have needed that! Louise Kelly and the Arvon gang for laughing at my silliness and joining SCBWI to become part of the scoobie gang.

Finally, the always there, the constantly supporting, the constantly encouraging, fabulous family of fairy godmothers: Geoff. Katherine. Christopher. They kept me going. They believed in me. Their pride in my achievement is too big to hug. But I'll try. I have long arms.